Boredom is Deadly

a novel by

Jackson Marlow

Printed in the United States of America

First Printing: June 2014

Published by: PULP21

ISBN-978-0-9905047-2-6

Dedication

To my partner in crime, LSH. You have a beautiful mind. Thank you for being there every step of the way.

Acknowledgments

Special thanks to *A lot of Cabernet Under the Bridge* Book Club, Gennady, Janet, John, KC, Kevin, and Sarah for their comments and suggestions. They were invaluable.

A Note to the Reader

Picture What You Read® is a unique niche format that specializes in fictional narratives accompanied by storyline photographs.   Visit the YouTube Channel: Picture What You Read® for Book Trailers, bonus material and unpublished photos from scenes in the book.

The eBook version of Boredom is Deadly contains vivid, HD color photographs.

Cast of Characters

The Victim and the Locals:

<u>Gillian Crawford</u>:   Young, rich and drop-dead gorgeous, with an IQ any think tank would love. Known for her peculiar demeanor, she spends her days on the island matching wits and charm with the local sheriff, priest and chef.   Her nights are a different story.

<u>Hadley Stevenson</u>:   Executive chef of the Boca Grande Hotel. He shares a secret past with Gillian. When he's not creating high-end cuisine for his guests, he's stirring up covert recipes with a dash of flair.

<u>Sam Mitchell</u>:   Local sheriff. Third generation law enforcement. Island's most eligible bachelor. Gillian gets under his skin more than he cares to admit.

<u>Lorelei Hampsted</u>:   Sheriff's secretary.   Gillian's distant cousin. They grew up together. Her feelings for the sheriff are as sweet as her famous pecan pie.

<u>Solomon Crawford</u>:   Retired, guarded, keeps mostly to himself.   Enjoys tinkering with his sailboat and fishing with Gillian. Same surname a coincidence; no relation.   Considers her the daughter he never had. His days are numbered.

<u>Father Francis Flannigan</u>:   Local priest, church league soccer coach, and paint by numbers hobbyist. He schools Gillian in the cause, reason and purpose

of life. She provides his parishioners anonymous solutions when legalities run amuck.

The Suspects:

<u>Philip Albright</u>: U.S. Marshal. Witness Protection Division. Sworn to serve and protect. He's gone missing, and his witness is dead.

<u>Boris Chenkov:</u> Moniker, the *Mad Russian*. Head of a Russian crime family. Wanted on three continents. Elusive. A chameleon. His partner, Vladimir Polinsky, has ratted him out, and he's seeking revenge.

<u>Yuri Glinka</u>: Chechnyan, with an ogre physique. Boris Chenkov's muscleman. Old school tactics.

<u>Nikolay Chenkov:</u> Creepy, computer hacker. Tall, pale, rarely sees the light of day. Youngest member of the Chenkov Family.

<u>Nadra and Homid Patel</u>: Islamic couple. Serious, guarded and ready to snap. He calls the shots. She trips on more than her burka while walking three steps behind.

<u>Katlyn and Cletus Wilcox</u>: Texans. Oil and real estate holdings. Nouveau-rich. He, loud and brash. She, the epitome of a trophy wife. Their stay is for business not pleasure, and timing is everything.

<u>Tilla and Johann VanBuren</u>: Elderly couple from upstate New York. Frugal and narcissistic. Inexperienced in concealing their European background, at least to the trained eye.

<u>Ralph and Rem VanBuren:</u> Twin grandsons of Tilla and Johann. Collegiate, with a sense of entitlement.

<u>Dennis Witherspoon</u>: Corporate executive on the mend. His bandaged face is fright-night worthy, or is he just incognito? No one knows for sure. Currently, his secretary is not taking appointments.

<u>Helen Crenshaw:</u> Androgynous power secretary for the rehabilitating and reclusive, Dennis Witherspoon. A close talker, and a people watcher.

<u>Christine and Brock Hansen</u>: The newlyweds. Corporate America. Comfortable being the center of attention. Her diamond ring would make a gemologist drool.

<u>Pauly Smith and Renzo Johnson</u>: Italian, connected, and smooth. Two wise guys laying low, per family orders.

<u>Harry Stevens</u>: The epitome of tall, dark and handsome. He gets what he wants. Subtle and obscure. Plays it close to the chest.

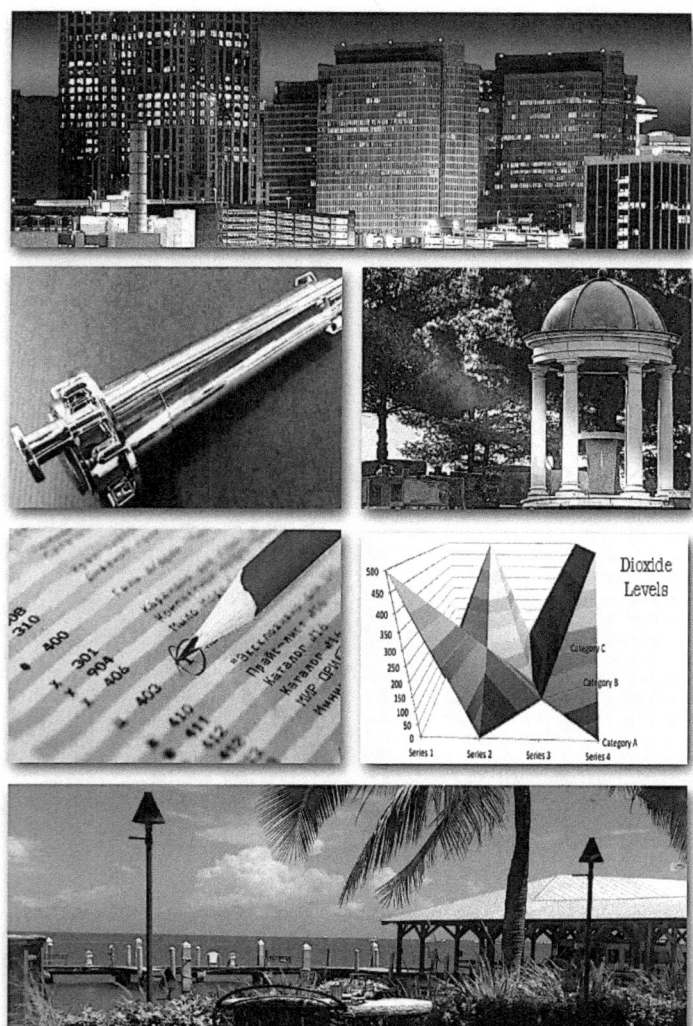

Chapter 1

"WE HAVE A situation, sir," blurted Agent Nick Bates of the U.S. Marshal's Service. The matter-of-fact statement he had practiced a half dozen times sounded a bit too anxious for his liking.

The grizzle-haired man sitting at the oversized mahogany desk glared annoyingly over his tortoise shell framed glasses. He had a cold and unsettling look; the kind that made people nervous and on edge from the get-go.

William T. Callaghan, a career man of thirty-five years, had a keen, calculating mind, an explosive disposition, and believed the politically correct scene was effectuated by a bunch of pansies.

Callaghan threw down his pencil, yanked off his reading glasses. "Define situation," he snapped, being clearly annoyed.

Bates, the rookie analyst, cleared his throat. The office air was warm and stale. A chewed off stogy laid smoldering in a stained, marble ashtray. He hated this part of the job. Kill the messenger came mostly to mind.

"One of our secretaries, a Rose Blackwood, had her purse stolen at the train station Friday night. She's assigned to Witness Protection on the fourth floor. We think she may have written her computer access code on a piece of scrap paper and placed it inside her wallet. There's reason to believe someone outside the agency has used her code."

"How high is her clearance," he shot back.

Bates swallowed gingerly. His face, now beaded with sweat, was flush like a seasoned alcoholic. "High enough to matter. She works for Albright." Bates locked the knees of his tenuous, six foot frame and waited for the reputational outburst.

Callaghan slammed his hands on the desktop and yelled, "How stupid can the ol' broad be? Call security. Yank her clearance, and kick her boney-ass out of here!"

"Yes, sir." Bates glanced at his notes in order to avoid further eye contact.

"Where the hell is Albright?" bellowed Callaghan, his Irish temper now fully loaded.

"He's on vacation, sir."

"Where?"

"We don't know. We're looking into his whereabouts. He hasn't checked in, in over seventy-two hours. Calls to his cell phone go directly to voice mail. No GPS. The SIM card has been either removed or damaged. He's gone off the grid."

Callaghan rubbed his fingers across a developing five o'clock shadow. "Continue," the old man growled as he snapped his pencil in two.

Bates glanced once again at his notes, then stuttered. "Yest ... yesterday, a security algorithm identified a suspicious access into one of our placement's files."

"What do you mean by suspicious?"

"Well, sir, once a placement's status code changes from new to seasoned, we have little need to further look at their file. Therefore, any time one of these older, seasoned files is accessed, the inquiry shows up on a suspect report, along with the employee's User ID. The auditing department contacts the employee and makes a few simple inquiries. When we first questioned Mrs. Blackwood, she denied any involvement. After several minutes on the hot seat, she disclosed the details of her stolen purse incident and confessed to the piece of scrap paper hidden in her wallet."

"Who's the placement?"

"His name is Vladimir Polinsky."

"Polinsky? Sounds Slavic. I don't remember him." His response and waving hand gesture suggested a sudden lack of interest.

Bates flipped through a few pages of notes and continued. "Vladimir Polinsky, our key witness in a diamond smuggling case involving the Russian Mafia two years ago. Before my time, sir."

Callaghan pointed his finger at Agent Bates. "Boris Chenkov, ex-party liner of the Soviet Union," he responded slowly, shaking his head. "Oh yeah, now I remember. Vladimir Polinsky, the supposed bean counter who promised to deliver Chenkov, aka the *Mad Russian*, in return for his sister's name being placed at the top of the US liver transplant list. Too much Russian vodka, I suppose." He cleared his throat and continued. "The deal waxed sweeter, given on the flip side, it involved a wealthy Brazilian, who was financing a Jihadist cell out of Munich. A guy named VonBuren. An Aryan thru-and-thru. Mossad still includes him on their watch list. Which is a polite way of saying, if they find him, they'll kill him."

"Come again?"

"Yeah, that's right. It's not enough we need to concern ourselves with Islamic extremists. I guess their hatred for the Infidel doesn't go as far as the Neo-Nazi movement. A strange connection exists between the Islamic extremists and Neo-Nazis we've yet to piece together. They're obviously both pissed off at us. We just need to connect the freakin' dots." His cynicism was clear as he rolled his eyes. "Hell, we've slept with our enemies more than I'd care to admit, all in the name of the ... greater good. Maybe that's it. They too have calculated the risk and are willing to turn a blind eye."

Bates had read enough case files from the Cold War Era to know just how true that statement really was. He nodded his head as he shifted his stance.

"Anyway, the transaction involved the sale of uncut, gem quality diamonds, the majority being pink from Brazil, which are rare I might add, in exchange for the guts to one of those missing Soviet nukes that were never delivered to central Russia for disarmament. Enough to make a dirty bomb or two."

"I'm afraid I didn't get that far in the write up, sir. What happened?"

Callaghan stared momentarily at the young agent and noticed the eagerness in his eyes, not unlike himself so many years ago.

He waved him to the chair. "Sit down, Mr. Bates. What I'm about to tell you was not one of our better days." Callaghan picked up the forgotten cigar, took a couple of puffs, and blew the smoke in the direction of the young agent. Bates wanted to fan it off, but didn't. Only Callaghan would find a loophole to E.O.13058.

"At the end of the Cold War, when the Soviet Union collapsed, the nuclear missiles from the fifteen Soviet Republics were to be shipped by land and sea to a central location for disarmament. Some from the Georgian Republic never arrived. No shocker there. Anyway, estimates are between 150 and 200 warheads unaccounted for. That royal screw up has obviously kept think tank analysts up nights, running what-if scenarios through their paranoiac heads. Anytime we get a chance to recover one, well, you can imagine."

"Yes, sir."

"It was called, *Operation Roundup*. A real black eye for the department. To begin with, no one knew what the maniac called the *Mad Russian* looked like. Sure, we had pictures of him twenty-five years ago, during the Cold War, but our intelligence told us he had extensive facial reconstruction, completely altering his appearance. No recent photos. A total new face. Therefore, our only option was to rely on Polinsky to ID him. Mistake number one. That never happened."

"Why not, sir?"

"Right when the parties started showing up, these street kids, local gang members, rode by on skateboards, and nailed the place with military grade smoke bombs. Visibility went down the toilet. Our agents jumped in with guns blazing. Mistake number two. Chaos ensued. People were running everywhere. A couple of our agents were shot, along with several of Chenkov's goons. When the smoke cleared, we had no Russian kingpin, no money man living large in Brazil, and no cache of diamonds."

"What about the nuclear material?"

"One birdcage recovered, with little inside."

"You mean the plutonium transport cage?"

"Yeah. Only one metal sphere weighing a tick under six kilos wrapped in a plastic bag and placed in a can filled with inert gas, which in turn is placed inside a cylinder known as the birdcage."

"So that was good." Bates was trying to sound optimistic.

"Not for what those diamonds were worth; not for what Polinsky led us to believe."

"Meaning, equitably there had to have been more, possibly another birdcage?"

"Precisely. Right in our grasp. Mistake number three."

"What about Polinsky? Did he give you a description of the *Mad Russian*?"

"Artist rendering, sure, but common opinion suggests he's altered his appearance again. That's when he's the most vulnerable though while he's convalescing. He's part of the Russian Mafia hierarchy, who are now extremely dangerous. They are technically more advanced than the Italian Mafioso, who some believe have lost their edge. One of their new favorites is to extort millions of dollars from charitable organizations during broadcasted pledge drives by sending fake traffic to their websites, which in turn crash because they can't handle the packaged bandwidth. As black marketers go, this guy's dossier includes the selling of guns, drugs, blood diamonds, women, and radioactive material to the highest bidder, including a Jihadist cell operating out of Germany."

"He's never been caught?"

"No. We believe he pretty much stays in Russia. Ever so often INTERPOL gets wind of him popping up in Eastern Europe or the Caribbean; however, it's always after the fact. The thing is, these Russian organized crime families live in an environment that is morally and legally corrupt. The country's virtually bankrupt, so the citizens suffer from basic governmental services. They steal from one another and trade commodities on the black market. It's a hot mess. With that kind of environment, organized crime thrives."

"An argument against free markets. Give me a classless society with shared benefits and resources, thank you very much."

Callaghan gave Agent Bates a cold stare.

"Poor characterization, ah ... sorry." Bates stammered.

Callaghan continued. "As for the Brazilian, Polinsky said it was a front man who brought the stones; an intellectual, well-schooled in physics. A heavy German accent. He asked the right questions and already had data readings showing the origin of the plutonium; a plant outside of Tbilisi, halfway between the Black and Caspian Seas."

Bates stepped in. "The dioxide readings. The enriched ore exhibits a unique mass fraction you can trace back to the plant."

"Exactly. Therefore, this was not their first time to meet."

"What about the diamonds?"

"The payment of choice for terrorists. Easy to transport, no electronic money trail, stabilized global asset value, and they don't set off metal detectors. These weren't your run of the mill either; the majority being pink. Each well over three carats in size. Worth about fifty million dollars."

"No sign of them?"

"Nope.   A lot of suspicion directed towards Polinsky though, since he was right there in the thick of things.   We had him under tight surveillance afterward, but nothing, not one clue or lead. He was a cool operator. I always had my doubts he was on the up and up, however he did help us take out a couple of the *Mad Russian's* key players, so we kept our word, and placed him under witness protection. Think we had to relocate him several times before he settled down somewhere.   Had to fake his death. There were a lot of people looking for him.   The Jihadists being particularly irate.   Nothing new on that account though."

"There's a chance the missing cache could still surface if we play our cards right." Agent Bates had a plan.

"Go on, I'm listening."   *Roundup* was a botched Op., thought Callaghan. It would be a major coup for the agency to acquire the material and redeem itself.

"Based on the security breach, under normal circumstances we would pull Polinsky in, then go through another relocation process. What if we were delayed in doing so, and he precipitately felt the need to take matters into his own hands? If he panicked, and indeed still had the goods, he just might reveal their whereabouts. If he were to flee, chances are he might go look for a fence. I say we send a team in to keep an eye on things. If the situation starts to heat up, we'll yank him. At any rate, Polinsky should be safe. This way, we might have a shot at recovering the stones or better yet, the ore."

"Bates, if your timing is off, you could be hanging him out to dry."

Agent Bates shrugged his shoulders. Callaghan's choice of pronouns was interesting.

There was a brief moment of silence between them.

"All right. Go ahead. But keep me informed."

"Yes, sir." Bates turned and reached for the doorknob.

"Bates," Callaghan growled.

"Yes, sir?"

"Where is Polinsky now?"

"We have him set up in a little town off the Southwest Florida coast called Boca Grande, under the alias Solomon Crawford."

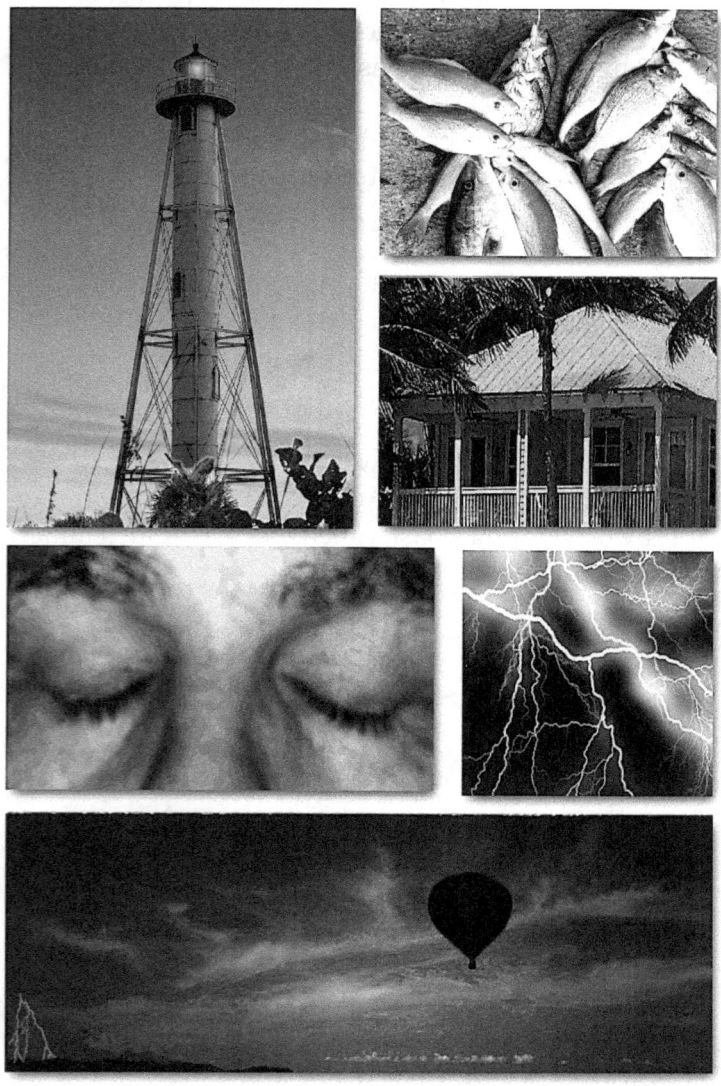

Chapter 2

Willie Ray Jones, head grounds keeper for the five star Boca Grande Hotel, shuffled through the stainless steel gourmet kitchen ready to call it a day. Being late in the evening, the kitchen had long since closed. From the center of the room, the hotel's chef de cuisine, Hadley Stevenson, glanced up and nodded.

"Hey, Boss," asked Willie Ray, in a thick, southern drawl, "ya' got some chik left?"

Hadley, who enjoyed the old man's company, responded in kind, "Venetian cinnamon, mellow Macadamia and Columbian deep roast. Take your pick."

Willie Ray rolled his aging brown eyes. "Freakin' rich folk," he muttered under his breath. He heard the term *'metro-sexual'* associated with the chef but remained confused as to its meaning.

Hadley chuckled and pointed to a large Viking stove. "Fresh pot of Maxwell House with your name on it. While you're here, help yourself to the leftovers from this afternoon's tea."

He poured himself a cup and sat down at the center prep table. At one end, dressed in a pristine white shirt and creased, black pants, sat a thirty-seven year old chef with impeccable credentials, stylish, handsome and self-assured. At the other end, sat a sixty-three year old black man, with deep cut wrinkles, dark green work khakis, and the smell of a hard day's work lingering close to his chest.

Willie Ray pulled a grungy white handkerchief

from his right hip pocket and wiped the back of his neck. Here it was mid-January, almost eleven o'clock at night, and the air was still crotch hot and sticky. He took a slow, easy sip of the refreshing brew and sighed in satisfying comfort.

"Whatcha' readin' there H?"

Hadley flipped to the front cover and held up the magazine. "Tropical Living," he said. "Not much to it, but they've published a short article about us on page eight."

"Surez nough? Whatzit say?"

He paraphrased. "Quaint village in Southwest Florida. Nestled between the twenty-sixth and twenty-seventh parallels; has a reputation for being a perfect getaway spot. Beautiful white powdered beaches, crystal clear blue waters, and trophy size fighting tarpon." He skimmed down the column with his finger. "At the southern tip of the island, beyond the Banyans and swaying Coco Plumosas, lies the Boca Grande Hotel; one of the country's few remaining Grande Dames. The historical treasure, like the Broadmoor or the Breakers, provides outstanding amenities - golf, tennis, pool, impeccably maintained croquet and polo fields, not to mention a first class restaurant, run by Hadley Stevenson, graduate of the Rue Leon Delhomme Le Cordon Bleu; known for his tantalizing seafood entrees and mouthwatering Key lime Pie. The hotel, owned by recluse philanthropist, Jonathan Alistair Cromwell, is a must stay for anyone on the winter vacation circuit."

Jones sat straight up looking proud as a peacock. "You get that, H? Im-pec-a-bly maintained croquet and polo fields. That's me. That's Mr. William Raymond Jones, thank you very much."

Hadley laughed as Willie Ray poked at his chest. He, on the other hand, could do without the publicity. Attention made his job much more difficult. Hadley glanced at his wristwatch, then reached for his keys.

"Guess I'll call it a day, Jonsey. Turn the stove and lights off when you leave." Hadley patted him on the back.

"Gotcha, Boss. I'll be leaving directly. Mind if I take the magazine home wit' me?"

"Help yourself, old man. Have a good one. See you in the morning."

ON THE OUTSKIRTS of town, a gray haired man in his early sixties, stood on the balcony of his whitewashed, yet weather worn beach house, gazing at the sky, mesmerized by its darkness. Dressed in a nappy white shirt and frayed khaki pants, he looked every bit the *'old guard'* as they were colloquially referred to. The masquerade had been effectively convincing, for he was anything but.

Solomon Crawford lived alone in a quiet neighborhood, on a dead end street. A section of cracker box bungalows set back off the road, surrounded by whispering pines.

Contiguous to his backyard was the pristine, white beachfront: sand dunes; sea oats. A popular backdrop for aspiring young artists, not to mention an attraction for the visiting snowbirds. For on the shoreline, the evening tide would deliver its nightly myriad of treasures, as sand dollars, sharks' teeth and coquinas arrived in welcomed abandonment.

In spite of the appeal Gasparilla Island had to offer, its beauty was unappreciated by him. Matters of consequence had left him with a feeling of sadness he could not shake. Even the double shot of vodka, imported from Mother Russia, did little to warm his empty soul. Sol's face, deeply tanned and wrinkled with age, showed many a laugh line. Evidence of how life once was. But not now. Not anymore. For the past twelve months, he had lived alone, in quiet seclusion, trying to make the most of his life, exiled in paradise.

Sol Crawford glanced at his watch: 12:30 a.m.

"One more hour," he commanded in a broken Russian accent. "After tonight, Boris, I will be calling the shots. You took my life, my family, now I will take yours."

For the past forty-eight hours that personal vendetta had been mulled over in his mind, and debated with his conscience. His time for revenge was near.

Several miles offshore, a thunderstorm approached. No rumbling yet, but lightning, lots of it, heating up the sky, looking for somewhere to strike. From the corner of Sol's porch, hanging from a dry rotted eave, wind chimes responded with an ethereal-like tune. Sea shells strung with five pound test. He tuned out the distraction. The comings and goings of the last two days were all he could think about.

His mind drifted to the Sunday edition of the Washington Herald. Buried deep on page six, above the fold was the headline that caught his eye: *'Russian Convict Escapes During Transit.'* He raced to the phone, grabbed the receiver, and punched in the memorized long distance phone number. Sol's contact, not at all pleased he had called on an open, unsecured line, assured him cryptically, that everything would be fine. His cover remained intact. There was no need to worry. *Were they naive or just plain* stupid, he wondered? Arkaidy Melovich had been one of Boris's key men. Head of logistics. Having him incarcerated would have hindered their illicit operations. With Melovich out of prison, they would be searching for him. A chill ran down his spine. Damn American Protection Program. No matter where they hid him, regardless of what new identity he employed, he knew the day would come when he would be face to face with that madman. No longer his comrade in arms, but instead, an enemy, his nemesis. God help him, and anyone that knew him.

The early paranoia returned. The wondering and waiting, always looking over his shoulder, forever looking at faces in the crowd, expecting at any moment to run into him, was making him crazy.

Regardless of what the agency said, he wasn't about to sit back and pretend everything remained status quo. He had one precious ace up his sleeve, referring to it encouragingly as his *'insurance.'* Before all was lost, he intended to cash it in; to be rid of Boris Chenkov once and for all. The call had been placed; the meeting set. There was less than an hour to wait. He was beginning to feel energized and in charge.

THUNDERHEADS WERE NOW close.

Rumbling. Booming. Bolts of lightning flickered across the darkening sky like nerve impulses carrying an electrical charge. Winds in the area had kicked up. It smelled like rain. Nightlife on the island was about to go inside.

A more perfect approach could not have been planned. Ominous storm clouds hid the anomaly from sight. With its black envelope and silenced propane burners, a small, hot air balloon drifted stealth-like across the sky.

As the two man balloon neared Sol Crawford's neighborhood, a male, dressed in black fatigues and night vision goggles, nodded to the pilot. Dangling over the side, his muscles flinched as the rope slipped in his hands. "How high," he yelled into the wind.

"Three thousand feet. Meet you on the other side."

In an instant, he was gone. The pilot watched the jumper in free fall until he opened his black chute. Feet soon on the ground. A quick hop. He, on the other hand, needed lift.

The exploding sound from the propane burners was essential to the next phase. Out of nowhere a German Shepherd came charging down the street, ready to wake the dead. His recon team had warned him and contingencies were in place: a t-bone steak laced with sedatives, wrapped in white, butcher paper. The pilot tossed the package in the direction of the street light, away from the strike zone. The canine took the bait, wagged his tail, and would soon be fast asleep.

Down the street, the paratrooper landed on the hard pavement without incident. He was fifty yards, at best, from Crawford's cottage. No neighborhood watchdog to bother him. He yanked off the parachute and stuffed it in a neighbor's trashcan. The morning pickup would take care of his gear before anyone was the wiser.

On cue, the burners ignited again, creating yet another distraction. The gondola, with its lone, anxious airman, slowly began its ascent. The pilot glanced at his watch. They were right on schedule. He adjusted the flames, turned around, and set his sights on the horizon.

At that moment, he realized what had happened. The storm had moved west, with no upward air currents to grab. He was too low. His present course amounted to collision and death - a tree line with sharp, broken limbs. The residual landscape following the last tropical storm.

The pilot snapped his safety belt to the metal frame and grabbed the railing. Their basket would take a beating. Probably be ripped to shreds. With any luck, the balloon itself would be spared, and the propane burners would stay lit. Otherwise, he was S.O.L.

As the gondola smashed through the trees, rocking the cage from side to side, the pilot lost his footing and crashed to the floor. The basket flipped sideways, dumping him over the edge, but the harness held tight, preventing his fall. He kicked and squirmed, struggling to get back inside. The clearing was close, less than fifty feet; their balloon, however, was but inches from being gouged. Suddenly, the basket took a dive, came upright, and flipped him back in. A huge limb crashed into the basket and jolted him against the tanks. The brass coupling for the fuel line broke loose, and in an instant the flame went out.

As the hot air balloon coasted along in silence, the pilot grabbed the propane switch and pulled on the trigger. The damp, evening air was working against him causing the ignitor not to light. He had no intention of ditching her into the black, choppy waters of the Gulf of Mexico, but the airship had begun its final descent. The sound of crashing waves onto the shoreline intensified. As he blocked the wind with his body, he turned the valve completely open and held the line. He could smell the propane. On the third click, came a loud blast. The balloon lit up like an enormous, incandescent black light bulb and began to climb.

The pilot emitted a sigh of relief. His heart was racing. Adrenaline rushed through his veins. He examined the basket. Two sides were damaged, but the frame would hold, at least for a short while. The transponder was activated. His chase team was standing by. A flashing green dot appeared on their LED screen. He was but a few minutes away. Onward he sailed.

Meanwhile on his back deck, Solomon Crawford scanned the dark, threatening sky, attempting to match sight with sound. A pattern of wind, silence, wind, silence. The diversion was an integral part of the plan.

The intruder entered the darkened bungalow, sight unseen. A reading lamp in the living room was the only light on. He did a quick study: navigational charts of Charlotte Harbor, black market Cuban cigars, unopened mail from a law firm in town, candid photographs of Polinsky and a young woman, one on a sailboat, the other from a fishing trip. He zeroed in on her face, making a note of several leads to follow.

With a cautious stride, he continued down the hallway and froze. A movement on the back deck stopped him cold. He returned his attention to the business at hand. To find stolen merchandise was one thing. To settle an old score was an entirely different matter.

Sol stood at the edge of the deck, his back to the house, hands on the railing, wondering where he'd be this time tomorrow night. He was so absorbed in his mental to-do list, he never heard his assailant's approach.

Slowly the hit-man advanced from behind, shortening the distance between them. At the edge of the deck, he hesitated, brushing his emotions aside. He knew his target and was surprised how much he'd changed. Polinsky had not aged well. Too old to be around much longer. A gratuitous endeavor. But orders were orders. When Polinsky stepped back from the railing, the moment was ripe.

The assailant grabbed him from behind, pinning his arms to his side. Sol panicked. He twisted and jerked like a fox in a steel trap, unable to break free. The assailant reached around with one arm and jabbed his thumb against his windpipe, cutting off his air supply. Sol kicked his legs as he gasped for air. In a moment, he would lose consciousness and black out. Frantic, he sank his teeth into his assailant's arm and punctured his skin. He could taste blood. His assailant flinched. That subtle reflex, though, was all Sol needed.

With the will of a desperate man, Sol reached up, grabbed the man's hair, yanked his head forward, and flung him over on his back. He was gaining momentum. Sol leaped through the air, body extended, in an effort to pin him down. The assailant, not to be counted out, raised his foot and landed a blow to Sol's crotch. He fell on his knees, moaning, struggling to swallow the bile that now rose in his throat. Again the assailant grabbed him from behind. This time Sol offered no struggle.

The last trace of adrenaline raced through his veins. Panic overtook his will to fight and survive. Through waves of anguish and misery he heard the assailant say, "Tell me ol' man, was betraying us worth it? Huh? Did you really think you'd be able to hide from us forever? Surely you knew we would never give up. Tell me where you stashed them, and I'll make this quick."

"I ... don't ... have ... them." Crawford's words were barely audible.

"You're such a fool Polinsky." He shook his head as an evil, vindictive look crossed his eyes. "Have it your way. Here's a bon voyage gift from Boris. He sends his regards, and said to tell you he'd see you in Hell."

It was quite easy for the long, thin blade of the stiletto to make its descent as he plunged the dagger between the ribs of his chest. Sol's breathing hitched. He tried to speak. Blood and bile spewed from his mouth. A pleading look filled his eyes as he shook his head, coughing, gagging. He knew the end was near and looked away. With a blank, unyielding face, the killer punched the blade into his chest and held it there - firm. The retaliating *coup de grace*. He watched indifferently as Sol's body stiffened and slowly exhaled his final breath. It was over. The deed was now done.

A thick stream of blood oozed from Sol's chest, staining the assailant's sleeve. He looked at his shirt and shook his head, annoyed and irritated. To dispose of evidence was always problematic. He yanked the stiletto out, through inches of ripped tissue and severed arteries then tossed him on the floor, void of all remorse. There on the wooden deck Sol remained: eyes glazed over, blood seeping out of his mouth and chest.

A look of rage filled the assailant's eyes as his nostrils flared and his chest heaved. His face was wild and frenzied, like a psychopath in the heat of passion. But the mood was soon gone. Within moments, he had regained a cool, distant facade. The persona of a hit-man; a cold-blooded killer. As he stood on the back deck staring down at his finished work, a look of satisfaction crept across his face, and a smug, almost sinister smile crossed his lips. He broke to the balcony's edge. At the railing, he turned around one last time and said in malicious pleasure, "You stupid old man. Diamonds or no diamonds, no one rats on Boris Chenkov and lives to tell about it."

Calculating the two story drop, he swung his long, steady legs over the railing and jumped. Once he made it to the beach, he stayed close to the water's edge, and took off running. High tide was on its way in - plenty of time to erase a would-be-welcomed trail.

SEVERAL HOURS PASSED. The breeze had virtually stopped and the incoming storm had moved south. The island paused in a blissful slumber. Only an hour or so remained before the first pale colors of the morning sky etched their way through the darkness.

Just before dawn, yet another man approached. Six feet plus in height, lean in frame, casually dressed. He snuck up through the dunes, remaining mostly in the shadows. He too had come a long way to see Sol.

Crawford's cottage was typical for island life. A landscape of ruby red bougainvillea and fragrant gardenia. Its bottom, or first floor, was mostly storage space and served as a garage. Three quarters of it was enclosed with latticework, the ornamental type, along with an outside staircase leading to the living quarters above.

The man ascended the wooden steps two at a time. A screen door at the top was locked. He popped the screen loose, reached in and freed the latch. Rusty hinges sounded off. He cursed his bad luck and quickly slipped inside.

The place was unnervingly silent. No sounds of life. He stood perfectly still while his eyes adjusted to the darkness. There was no immediate indication as to what happened to Sol.

They were to meet at the island's lighthouse at 1:30 am. The old place had been put to rest years ago, remaining only now as a landmark. Located on the south end of the island, off Gasparilla Drive, it was a couple of miles from the main drag. Late at night, the old road was lightly traveled, making for a private, out of the way place to meet. Sol had called the meeting, saying it was urgent. He never showed. Something had gone wrong. After waiting for over an hour, he decided to take a look around. Sol's beach house seemed the logical place to start.

As he turned the corner towards the kitchen, something crunched under his left foot and darted in front of his eyes. He dove to the floor, yanked a 9mm Beretta from his belt, injected a cartridge into the chamber and froze, not daring to breathe. He could feel his heart pounding and his pulse racing. A bead of sweat rolled down the side of his face. A house cat, the Persian type, darted for the hallway.

Slowly he stood, right finger still on the trigger as he studied the room. Sol's place was cozy, not elegant, with stacks of books and old newspapers all in messy piles. Big, overstuffed sofas and chairs filled the rooms. Next to the limestone fireplace, standard in houses this old, yet seldom used, was a black, baby grand. Its top was down. In the center were photographs framed in beveled glass. He walked over and lifted one. It seemed to be out of line with the rest. The picture was of Sol and a young woman, both smiling in front of a motley display of what he presumed was their catch of the day: snapper, mackerel and yellowtail.

She was disturbingly attractive, with shoulder length brown hair, and large doe-like eyes. He didn't recognize her. No surprise though. Not someone from Sol's past. Probably someone he'd met on the island. He returned the frame to its original skewed position, then headed for the back deck.

It was then that he spotted a body lying face down on the wooden floor, and rushed over to its side. Carefully he rolled the figure over, already expecting the worst. Sol was lying in a pool of blood. He touched his face. His skin was ice cold, and ashen gray. Rigor mortis had begun to set in.

"I've had no contact with you in over two years, and now this?" He shook his head. Disgusted. "What a waste," he said with a sigh. He knelt down and placed a hand over Sol's haunting dead eyes, then somberly pulled his eyelids forever closed.

He slowly stood, teeth clenched, jawbones tightened, anger swelled inside. His mind raced in a thousand directions. *How the hell did Boris Chenkov find him? What happened? Sol must have suspected something. That would explain why he risked his anonymity and wanted his help. He would need serious money and resources to truly disappear. Sol hardly had the means, or did he? No time to think about that now. Others might be watching.* He wiped the edges of the picture frame clean, smeared the door handle with his jacket, then raced down the stairs. *Too bad he had moved the body.*

Chapter 3

Straight up 5 a.m., the telephone rang. Gillian Crawford was jolted out of bed. Good news would never call at this ungodly hour, she sighed. Her mind was numb. She cleared her throat and answered it on the third ring.

"Yes, hello."

"Did I wake you, dear?" asked the elderly gentleman on the other end.

"Not quite," she responded, reaching for the alarm clock and focusing on the time. "Is everything all right?" she asked, trying to sound coherent. Doubting not, she waited for his reply. Jonathan Alistair Cromwell, philanthropist, and maternal uncle would never call to chit-chat.

"I have a proposition for you."

"Now, Uncle Jack," Gillian moaned but was cut off.

"Before you get too far into your sanctimonious speech about being out of the business, let me say I would consider this a personal favor. Besides, even though you deny it, you're like your father. You feed on the danger. This cloak and dagger stuff is in your blood."

She caved. "All right. What is it this time?"

"I know someone who needs a hundred thousand in a hurry. The next day or two preferably. The usual channels are unavailable, and I cannot be involved. Can you do this, my dear?"

Gillian, wide awake now, rubbed her throbbing forehead and sighed, "Yes, I'll take care of everything.

Any preference this time?"

"Hmm ... I'd rather like something with football."

Gillian smiled bleakly. "All right, Uncle Jack. I'll see what I can do. I'll call you when I'm done."

"Splendid, my dear. I knew I could count on you." Click went the line as he hung up.

Gillian, who still held the receiver in her hand, responded sarcastically, "You're welcome." Knowing full well, her uncle would never say thank you.

TWO HOURS LATER, Gillian Crawford sat at her desk looking at an incredible vista of the Gulf of Mexico from her beachfront estate. Late twenties, rich, good looking, educated at Oxford, with a 169 IQ. She was easily bored with too much time on her hands. There lied the problem. She glanced at her watch and dialed the phone number to the Boca Grande Hotel's kitchen.

"Hadley, it's me."

"Bonjour, mademoiselle. You're up early."

"I need to run a quick errand." Having worked together for many years, he knew exactly what the words *'quick errand'* meant.

"Ahh ... I thought we had both retired."

"Your Boss called me this morning and made a personal request."

"Of course he did." When the name, Jonathan Alistair Cromwell, was mentioned, he was all business.

"Can you meet me by the delivery door in about an hour? I need something airborne, potent, but not lethal."

"I think I can come up with something. Call me

when you head out. I'll go outside for a smoke break."

"Thanks, Hadley. I owe you." Gillian hung up the phone then navigated through several Internet sites booking a series of flights.

Back in her bedroom, she threw some clothes into an overnight bag, then proceeded to open a wall safe behind an original Chagall painting. Gillian grabbed five strapped stacks of twenty dollar bills, slammed the door and spun the dial.

As she headed down the hallway to the living room, she heard an all too familiar sound that made her smile. "I'm coming, Ollie. I'm coming. Hang on a second." She walked over to a large steel cage and yanked off a white silk cover.

"Good morning, sweetie. How are you this morning?" She rubbed the parrot's chest with her finger. Ollie was the one and only love of her life. Her sole commitment. On days when she struggled with purpose and existentialism, he provided a simple focus, and was always glad to see her. *Kind of like a dog, but without the fleas,* she thought.

"Want some pistachios before I head out? I'll be gone for a couple of days, so you hold down the fort, okay? Here, give me a kiss." She leaned her face to the cage while Ollie pecked the end of her nose.

Gillian headed to the garage, threw her bag into the back of her vintage 1957 MG, got in and cranked it up. First gear was always a little rough. She eased down the long driveway of her estate, opened the electronic ten foot iron gate and took off.

Five minutes later, she pulled into the side parking lot of the grand hotel and spotted Hadley leaning up against a Royal Palm having a smoke. *The guy was too smooth for his own good,* she chuckled to herself.

Hadley walked over to the car and handed her a large pair of field binoculars. Gillian looked at them with a quizzical eye.

"Sometimes I amaze myself," he said with a laugh.

"Where is it?" Gillian asked.

"Stored behind the lens. Simply turn the chamber until you hear a click and the left side will pop open. You'll need to check your bag, though. The airport screeners will pick it up."

Gillian tested the chamber and spotted the hidden vial.

"Whatever you do, don't drop it. You won't like this bug if you catch it, understood?"

"Gotcha," she replied. "The guys up north would be proud."

"I aim to please. When will you be back?"

"Day after tomorrow."

"See you then. Be safe, mon cheri."

SEVEN HOURS LATER, a maid with a push cart, scuffled down the hallway of a posh New Orleans hotel; host to one of this year's collegiate football teams, playing for the national championship. With gray, wiry hair, saggy breasts, and an oversized rump, she was all but invisible during the mid-afternoon hours following the hotel's check-out time.

The maid reached into her apron pocket for the master key and knocked on the door to Room 707. No one answered. She entered and shook her head -

bombshell. Clothes on the floor, lamp and ceiling fan. Last night's room service tray in the bathtub. Back to her cart she checked the clipboard one more time to verify the guest's name: starting quarterback for the favored returning champs, playing tomorrow for a national title. She then closed the door and engaged the dead bolt.

Thirty minutes later, with his room in order, she reached into her pockets, took out a mask, a Petri dish and a Phillips-head screwdriver. With the mask secured over her nose and mouth, she stood on a chair, removed the air conditioning register and placed the Petri dish inside the vent. She steadied her hands. Suddenly, there was a knock at the door as someone fumbled with the handle. Her heart skipped a beat. She hopped down and went to the door. Through its peephole, she spotted a blonde haired groupie wearing a tight fitted pink t-shirt and short denim mini-skirt.

"Please don't have a key card," she whispered to herself.

There was another knock and failed attempt at the door handle. Annoyed at her diminishing prospects, the girl finally gave up and left.

The maid climbed back on the chair and carefully removed the top of the Petri dish. She studied the culture for a moment. The virus had multiplied. She screwed the register back in place, then cranked the thermostat up to 90 degrees. *Nasty germ that one,* she said to herself. *He will feel like hell for a few days but will recover. Too bad his team wouldn't.* She placed a complimentary chocolate on his bed and shut the door.

A UNIFORMED DOORMAN, impeccably dressed, opened the front door to Caesar's Palace in Las Vegas. Gillian, in a little red dress and Louboutin stiletto heels, made her way to the sports room. She studied the posted odds, 15:1, then looked at the time. The team captains were a few minutes away from the coin toss. *A ten thousand dollar bet should do the trick,* she thought. With her wager placed, she grabbed a table in an adjoining lounge and ordered a vodka martini with two olives. The sports bar was full of HD televisions, covering a myriad of sporting events, with the Jumbotron, front and center, carrying the championship game live. Talking heads were buzzing with news. The top recruited QB had not returned from the locker room. An unconfirmed case of influenza. He would not play in tonight's game. The odds on the wager board flipped in her favor.

Three hours and two martinis later, shocker, the underdogs won. She cashed in for one hundred fifty thousand dollars, then caught a cab to the airport.

As Gillian waited for her flight out of McCarran International, she dialed an unlisted number from her cell phone, then paced the gate area while the call connected.

The voice on the other end asked, "Did you have any problems?"

"No, sir. Went off without a hitch."

"Very well. I'll have a courier pick up the cash later tomorrow. Those tickets you asked for were delivered to your house this morning."

"Thank you. I appreciate it."

"You're welcome" He hung up before she could respond.

Gillian disconnected the SIM card from her cell phone and tossed it in a trash can. On the plane ride home, she sat in first class, with no one beside her. A flight attendant brought her a cola with ice. Two headache powders later, she closed her eyes and prayed for some relief.

Chapter 4

Gillian Crawford parked her car in a shady spot at the Boca Grande Hotel, ready for breakfast. It was 9 o'clock of the next day. No fan of cooking, she frequented the hotel's restaurant each morning for some of Hadley's savory fare. The coffee wasn't half bad either.

As she approached the hotel's porte-cochere, the distant sound of an emergency siren piqued her interest. Not uncommon, given the number of retirees on the island, but this time it made her feel anxious and uneasy. Maybe if Sam showed his face at breakfast, he would fill her in on the details.

Sam Mitchell, the town's law-and-order, was born and raised on the island; a detail they had in common. He was third generation law enforcement, Gillian's neighbor and contemporary. They disagreed on most things, but managed to enjoy each other's company nonetheless.

The island's police force was a three man operation: Sam, the sheriff, a deputy by the name of Gus Lambert, who moonlighted as a commercial fisherman, and Lorelei Hampsted, their secretary. Crime on the island was minimal, which suited the town folk and Sam just fine. He had the makings of a good ol' boy, was inquisitive when he needed to be, and thought Gillian was a conundrum he had yet to figure out.

There was a history between them they didn't talk about. With both being attractive and single, their names were frequently in the mix. Small town stuff.

People loved to gossip, especially about the Mitchell and Crawford families.

Two years ago, Gillian's parents were killed in a boating accident. Their motor yacht had a damaged fuel line and exploded. During the memorial service, Gillian had to be guided through the motions. She never once shed a tear.

When the day was over, and the last of the condolences delivered, Gillian snapped out of the fog. The emptiness she felt was unbearable. She walked out on the beach, sat alone in the sand, and had a long, hard cry; 18 year old scotch at her side.

Later that evening, Sam Mitchell came by to check on her and found her passed out with her face in the sand; cold, wet and shivering. He picked her up, held her in his arms and carried her inside. In the bathroom, he stripped off her wet clothes, turned on the hot water and placed her in the bathtub. Moments later, her eyes still closed, Gillian mumbled his name and smiled. He stayed the night, through the nightmares, the sobbing, the talking in her sleep. In the morning, he was gone. The incident was never brought up again - like it never happened.

GILLIAN ENTERED THE restaurant and discreetly scanned the room. An old habit that was hard to break. The maître d' showed her to her usual table, a location in the corner, and helped her with her chair. It offered the perfect vantage point; she had chosen well.

Throughout the social season, the hotel rooms ran eight hundred dollars a night. Guests this time of the year were a rich, motley crew, from all walks of life, with eccentricities to match. She settled in for her first cup of coffee, and proceeded to sharpen her *sherlockian* skills.

From the adjacent window, she could see the croquet course. Its grass was lush and green this time of year. Several hotel guests were up early to enjoy a round of the old lawn game. Mahogany mallets, bright painted wooden balls, the required white attire, a little wagering to make the outing interesting. Later in the day they would relax under the green and white striped tents, drink fruity concoctions laced with Jamaican rum, and eat authentic yellow, key lime pie; contrary to the notion it was supposed to be pea green.

The waitress handed her a menu. "Busy morning, Miss Gillian."

"Yes, I noticed the crowd. Looks like only a few tables available."

"A fishing tournament. First one this year. I believe Snook are running." The waitress wrote down her order.

On mornings like this, the patrons were mostly men. Very few women were up to the rough, choppy waters of Boca Grande Pass. Deep water, big fish. Instead, you would see them shopping in the quaint boutiques or art galleries located in the center of town or better yet, down at poolside, soaking up the sun with teenage cabana boys at their beck and call. Later, between the hours of three and four, they would patronize the restaurant, fashionably dressed, when high tea was served. The creme brûlée was to die for.

Gillian glanced slowly around the dining area,

looking for a place to start. In the center of the room was a young man and woman she labeled Corporate America: sales, no tans, badly in need of a vacation. She was stunning, and he was near a dime. Everything they wore, from the Dolce and Gabbana sunglasses to their John Lobb suede driving shoes appeared brand new. Closets full of thousand dollar suits, but no casual wear. They seemed to enjoy the spotlight, hence commanding the coveted center table. He had dark hair, dark eyes, mid-thirties, give or take, with a smug look on his face. His expression: nothing short of a house cat who had just swallowed a canary. She, the canary, had shiny, platinum blonde hair, recently dyed, pulled up in a bun, in order to favorably display her stunning face: high cheekbones, slim nose, large blue eyes, full red lips. Gillian couldn't help but notice the enormous diamond ring weighing down her left hand, as she fidgeted with the platinum setting. *Must be newly placed,* she decided. No ring for him. She noticed his left hand remained gripped to a glass of ice water, as if trying to cool it down. Both had ordered a big breakfast. No doubt the previous evening's activities had spurred their appetites.

Gillian glanced to her left. Three tables over could be that same couple forty years later; the lustfulness being replaced by a more comfortable, endearing demeanor attained only by many years of marriage. A rarity to be sure. She guessed they were both in their early seventies. He had a large stomach which hung decisively over his belt. A beer man. Thick, white hair, no glasses. His feet bothered him. Function had won out over style. His wide toe, white leather, tennis shoes were fairly worn. She had thick, frameless glasses, a questionable dye job, the color somewhat blue, wore a plain pink blouse and blue skirt, classic wardrobe, impeccable quality, with a mouth that never stopped. Not big eaters. Forks upside down in their left hand. Tea, not coffee, with scones and jam. European. He seemed preoccupied with the newspaper, but managed to nod occasionally so as to appease his wife that he was indeed still listening.

That changed when two young men approached their table. Tall, blonde, collegiate. They each gave the woman a peck on the cheek and shook the gentleman's hand. Judging by their age, and fond regard, she guessed they were their grandsons. All four shared an air of self-importance, their posture above reproach, their manners, spot on. The elderly couple listened as the two young men communicated an anecdotal account that appeared serious. *Serious being a relative term,* she thought. Their voices remained low, impossible to overhear from where she was seated. Their concerns, probably nothing more than the money they needed from their grandfather to charter a fishing boat. By their equal need for haircuts, she guessed their stay here was of a sudden nature. And given their sunburned necks, they had already spent one day out on the water.

On the far side of the room, sitting alone, was the most interesting subject yet: an older woman who seemed completely out of place. She wore a beige, business suit with a paisley necktie. The androgynous look. Next to her plate was a yellow legal size pad of paper on which she would hastily write. Her hair was short, dull, razor cut, possibly a wig. She wore only a tad of lipstick, and managed to balance a pair of black frame glasses onto the bridge of her wide, hooked nose. A people watcher like herself, Gillian realized, although why she was taking notes, was beyond her. Her face was downcast, however her beady, brown eyes stayed busy as they shifted side to side. At the moment, she seemed particularly interested in a gentleman sitting alone, two tables to her left, reading the morning newspaper. A bad angle for Gillian to discern much more.

All of a sudden, the woman put down her pencil, glanced at her watch, and snapped her fingers descriptively calling for her waitress. Gillian strained her ears in order to hear.

"I would like for you to send a carafe of fresh squeezed orange juice, not some frozen concentrate, along with a pot of coffee, and a pastry tray to Mr. Witherspoon's suite, 203. Please confirm the coffee is hot and black, and tell the busboy to not be alarmed by the bandages, nor to acknowledge them in his presence. He is convalescing from a car accident.

Knowing the layout of the hotel, Gillian knew Suite 203 was one of the larger ones in the east wing. Mr. Witherspoon must be her boss. Convalescing in a resort hotel room you didn't venture from seemed odd. She tagged her as one of those power secretaries: protective, and a control freak. She knew the type. Uncle Jack had one. She kept the one word description she had in mind to herself.

Breakfast arrived. This morning's fare was

Belgian waffles laden with strawberries and sweet cream. For Gillian, it was a means to camouflage her activity. Her eyes scoured the opposite corner of the room without much interest. Then she spotted him. She laid down her fork. This one had deviant eyes. No soul. The young man's unsettling gaze was locked on hers. He gave her the once over, then nodded his head in greeting. Gillian managed a thin smile before lowering her head. Her hands began to fidget.

The creeper was in his mid-twenties, pale, thin, spiked brown hair, chapped lips, with a disturbing aura. A junkie or computer freak, she decided. Didn't get out much, stayed jacked up on caffeine, drank little water, dehydrated, an occupational consequence. *Why would someone like him be here,* she wondered.

He sat at a table with an older man, mid-forties, whose large frame and features were hard to overlook. Orge-ish, but not vulgar. The man had a low, rich laugh, which commanded attention. He typified the sort who lived life to the fullest. Judging by the gold jewelry he wore around his fingers, wrists and neck, he could easily afford to.

It was now the peak time for breakfast, and the last three tables were taken. The first hosted an Arab couple. Both young, he in khakis, she in a blue burka, not exactly suitable attire for Florida's humidity. No bacon for them.

She had black, smoldering eyes, as remote as eyes could be. Arranged marriage, no doubt. He had a leaden face, with pinched nostrils and sunken temples. Odd to see Arabs here on vacation. *What was up with that,* she wondered. The Middle East seemed more their destination of choice. Pilgrimage to the land of their Persian ancestors. *Inshallah. What Allah wills.* They were here for a reason, although she doubted it was to soak up the sun.

At the second to the last table, the male guest had to be a Texan. His loud mouth and lack of table manners added up to poor breading and new money. He sported ostrich boots, a Stetson hat, which he failed to check at the door, and a pink clad trophy wife hanging on his every word. She was accessorized with big hair, heavy highlights, significant breasts, and a cooler size, unzipped, Louie Vuitton purse lying on the table. *Why did they never zip them,* Gillian wondered.

The patrons at the last table, located directly in front of her, had obviously bathed this morning in Armani cologne. Hawaiian shirts, shiny black hair. Their ability to mainline espresso and devour a plate of cannolis in a heartbeat seemed likely. Minus the dropped 'g' in their speech, she gathered they were from Brooklyn, and were here to make someone an offer. She shook her head. That was too cheesy for even her to finish. Regardless of their line of work, the one with the crooked nose was definitely worth a second glance. She sighed without realizing.

By the third cup of coffee, Gillian was put out. Sam had yet to arrive, and her curiosity was getting the best of her. Her waitress stopped by and offered her another refill.

"No thanks, Emma. I'm done. Let me borrow your pen and I'll sign the receipt."

"Already been taken care of, Miss Gillian."

"Excuse me?"

"Yes, ma'am. Nice tip, too." Emma pulled a fifty dollar bill out of her uniform pants pocket.

"By whom?"

"By that man walking out the side exit," she replied, nodding discretely to the glass door.

Gillian spun around. Carmine and Vinnie, as she immediately coined them, were strutting out the door. She grabbed her purse to head their way. Halfway across the room she stopped.

Sam entered. By his appearance, he had pulled an all-nighter. Gillian had that same uneasy feeling return.

"Sam, you look bloody awful." Gillian, direct as usual, was one of the few people that called him by his first name. To everyone else, he was 'Sheriff.'

There was nothing in that for him, so he ignored the jab.

He scoured the room, frowned, then pointed to her table in the corner.

"Fishing tournament," she said, answering his unspoken question.

"Right," he replied, but said nothing more. Sam pulled out a chair, sat down and sighed. A waitress came over and poured him some coffee.

"The usual, Sheriff?"

He was clearly not thinking about breakfast at the moment and hesitated. "Uh, yes, ma'am, thank you." His fingers thumped the table.

"So, what's up? I heard an ambulance siren this morning. Does it have anything to do with that?"

He rubbed the whiskers on his face. "Solomon Crawford is what's up, Gillian," he began. "Lorelei received a 911 call earlier this morning from his housekeeper, Miss Sarah Mae. She was hysterical. Apparently she walked in at her usual time, and found him lying on the back deck."

Gillian became very still. "What happened? Is he all right?"

Sam hesitated, hating to tell her. He reached for her hands and held them in his. The affection struck her odd. It was out of character, particularly lately. He was making her uncomfortable.

"What, Sam? Just tell me." With a lump now in her throat and her heart racing, she braced herself for the news.

"He's dead, Gillian. Murdered."

"Murdered?" she uttered. "No, no, that's crazy." She pulled her hands away.

He gave her a stern look, nodded his head, then glanced around the room.

"A press conference is scheduled for noon today. Not public knowledge yet. I came over after things settled down, so I could tell you personally. I know he was pretty much a hermit, but still, you knew him better than anyone else."

Gillian slumped in her chair, stunned. Her eyes welled up. She shook her head, and squeezed her nose, while trying to hold back the tears. Sam remained silent and waited. He knew he had opened up some pretty painful memories. Ever since her parents' death, she had been unwilling to let anyone get close, including him. Mr. Crawford seemed to be the same, although the reason for his standoffish demeanor was not known. Strangely enough, that commonality seemed to ignite their friendship. Now, once again, someone Gillian had cared for was dead.

This time, murdered.

"I'm sorry."

Gillian raised her head and nodded. "How?"

"Stabbed in the chest. He bled out. What a sight. Sarah Mae will never be the same. Doesn't appear to be robbery though. The M.E. said time of death was thirty-six hours ago, give or take."

"I can't believe this. I just saw him a day or two ago at the marina. He was working on his boat."

"Did he seem okay at the time? Anything bothering him?"

Gillian rubbed her throat, trying to ease the tightness. "Not that I recall," she replied. "I guess you knew he didn't like to talk about himself, or his past for that matter. I pushed the subject once, and he got belligerent. I apologized. After that, we stuck to politics, the weather, and fishing."

"Could be his past finally caught up with him."

"Rather callous thing to say, don't you think?"

He ignored her. "What about out of town friends?"

He never mentioned anyone from out of ... ." Gillian's voice dropped off, and a faraway look filled her eyes.

"Wait a second." She snapped her fingers. "There was someone. Now what was his name? Max, something."

"That's helpful," Sam replied sarcastically.

"Shut up. I'm trying to remember." She tapped her forehead with her fingers. "I spotted a newspaper lying on Sol's kitchen counter a while back. It was the classifieds, the personal ads, and several were circled in red." Gillian shook her head up and down as she recalled the words. "Yeah, now I remember. Sol nonchalantly picked it up and threw it in the trash can after he noticed my interest. I had a solid look though before he did. It was a message to Sol from a Max Taylor."

Her talent for absorbing details always amazed him. "You know, you shouldn't go around reading other people's mail and such. Someone might question your upbringing."

"Funny."

"One of these days that inquisitive nose of yours is going to get you in trouble, and I'm not going to be around to save you. Take up a hobby to fight the boredom, why don't you?"

"We've had this conversation before," she snapped back. "Do you want this information or not?"

"By all means," he threw up his hands signaling a truce. "Go right ahead. I'm all ears."

"Now where was I? Oh, yes. It was the classified ad section of the Washington Herald. The message was cryptic. Four or five ads had several words underlined from each circled post. When you read them from top to bottom, it said, *'Safety net ripped. Stay alert. Max Taylor.'* Strange message, don't you think? I mean, why wouldn't this Taylor fellow just pick up the phone, or drop him a line, unless ... ." Gillian hesitated again, this time with a gleam in her eyes. "Unless he didn't know how to reach him because Sol was in hiding. Yeah, that would make sense. Let me see what I can find out."

"No," Sam shot back, holding his hand up like a stop sign. "I'll take it from here. Besides, I seriously doubt '*Max Taylor*' is his real name. I've never heard of anyone using their real name in personal ads."

"Oh, so you're familiar with them, are you? Let me guess, *Single White Male seeks Straight White Female, high school education a plus, willingness to cook, clean and walk three steps behind preferred.*"

"That's enough, Gillian." His voice was direct, and condescending. "Now you listen to me. You are not to get involved with this, in any way, shape or form, do you understand?"

"Why, because it might be too dangerous?" Her sarcasm was as sharp as a blade.

"As a matter of fact, yes." The veins in his forehead were now bulging.

"Oh, please. I'm not some helpless, little female, you know."

"Now darlin', don't get your panties in a knot. I was just ... ."

"Just forget it," she blurted out, as she slammed her fist on the table. "And don't call me darlin'." The retort came out much louder than she had intended. She threw back her hair, grabbed her purse, and stormed out the door.

There was an awkward pause in the dining room's chit-chat. The sheriff straightened his tie and cleared his throat.

Two tables down, the '*bad angle*' male guest peeked over his newspaper. Until now, he appeared to be occupied with the business section of the Miami Ledger, but in truth, had been observing the lady with the temper. Many a head turned when she walked out of the restaurant. He guessed the sound of tires squealing out front belonged to her, as well.

No doubt, the conversation she had with the police officer still sitting at her table had gotten her steamed. Based on how he was stabbing his steak and eggs, he didn't seem too jazzed either.

He had spent the last half hour studying her face. She was the woman in the photograph on Vladimir's piano. A real distraction that one. He wondered how she was tied to this, and just how much she really knew. He glanced quickly around the room. It was a small town; someone would give up the dirt.

Just then his waitress appeared. She checked the charge receipt before handing it to him to sign. "Thank you, Mr. Stevens. Anything else I can get you?"

He folded the newspaper, looked up and smiled. His was the kind of smile women couldn't get enough of. "Why yes, there is, as a matter of fact."

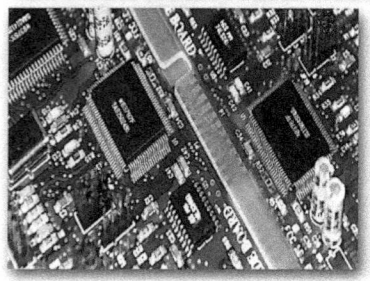

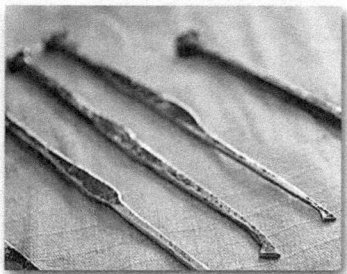

Chapter 5

Parked on the shoulder of the beach access road, was an ordinary white cargo van; dark tinted windows, orange traffic cones scattered about, a metal ladder on top. Inside housed a built-out surveillance center equipped with state-of-the-art monitors, transmitters, and laptops.

A phone call halted the occupant's work.

"Pack up and get out. I'm at the restaurant. She just left."

"Okay. We're about finished."

The technician in charge jumped out of the van. A direct link connected him instantly to a member of his team inside Gillian Crawford's estate.

"What do you need," answered the guy on the other end; annoyed by the phone chirp.

"She's on her way. You've got three minutes tops."

"Are we up?"

"Yes, I've got a live feed. Now get the hell out."

The man inside whistled to his crew of three. He motioned his hand across his throat. They hurried with the final adjustments to the ceiling fan, phone receiver and flower arrangements.

Ollie, the parrot, squawked loudly and flapped his wings.

"Shut up, bird," one of them yelled. He punched the cage with his fist. It wobbled back and forth but did not tip over.

A cursory look by the man in charge confirmed all was back in place. They rushed out the side door and ran to the concrete wall: six feet high, with motion sensors every twelve feet. No small leap, as they helped each other over the top. They remotely re-activated the alarm when all was clear.

Meanwhile, two guys jumped out of the van. One slapped a magnetic decal on the driver's side door, while the other arranged orange cones around the manhole cover. A moment later, a maroon MG downshifted and eased into the driveway.

Gillian paid a passing glance at the truck. Fiber optics company. Typical: three guys standing around while one was working.

She entered her house a moment later. The telephone rang.

"Gillian, it's Lorelei."

"Morning, cuz. So he called you in to work today, huh?" Gillian had glanced at the caller ID. Lorelei was family. A distant cousin on her mom's side, who had it bad for the sheriff.

"I'm calling to tell you how sorry I am about Mr. Crawford's passing."

"Thank ... you," Gillian answered in a staccato like fashion, as if her brain and speech were disjointed. "Yes ... terrible news ... can't imagine why someone would do that." Not in the mood for a female bonding session, she quickly changed the subject. "Is the sheriff around?"

"He just left. He was here at the station for only a few minutes when another call came in. There's a fatality at the toll bridge. They've called for a tow truck and ambulance."

"Really?" Gillian responded. Her curiosity piqued. First Sol, now this.

"Yeah, and boy is he in a foul mood, so watch out."

Gillian re-lived her earlier flair up with him, in silence, as her head took on a bobble head effect. She regretted Lorelei had been the recipient of his ill temper. Especially since she was the reason, and Lorelei, the innocent bystander.

"I was getting ready to leave, sweetie, when you rang. Can I get back with you later?"

"Of course. Whenever you need to talk, I'm here. I best get back to this mountain of paperwork he gave me. Call me, Gillian, if you need anything, okay?"

"I will," she responded and quickly hung up the phone. She had no time for this.

Gillian sat at her desk and ripped off a cryptic email to Uncle Jack, inquiring as to one Solomon Crawford and a Max Taylor out of D.C. After that she picked up the phone, dialed 411, got the number to Linkco Fiberoptic Systems, and was connected. Inside the surveillance van, the phone rang.

"Here we go," one of the younger guys said.

"Linkco, how may I direct your call?"

"Yes, I'm calling about a road crew on East Shore Drive, in Boca Grande.""One moment, please. I'll connect you to customer service." The man with the headset put her on hold. "She's quick. You ready?" he asked the man sitting next to him.

"I'm ready. Put her through."

Gillian received a scripted response to the work being done, which seemed to satisfy her. The team watched through the video feed as she walked around her living room. She stopped by the birdcage and looked down at the floor: a wet spot and a stray feather on the carpet.

The crew looked at the guy who hit the cage, and shook their heads.

"You guys are getting sloppy," said the one in charge. "First you almost blew the security alarm, then, as if nothing of consequence was in play, you took your sweet time putting in a few surveillance bugs, and video cams."

"We didn't plan on a ten digit access code, for one thing," replied the leader of the inside team. "And look at that encryption. You can't get through, can you? Either she has something pretty valuable inside, or she's been in the business. That's not some ordinary set up you're looking at."

SIX MILES UP the road, Gillian arrived at the accident site. Traffic was backed up on both sides of the bridge. Sun worshippers arriving, rubberneckers leaving. Gus directed traffic while the sheriff talked with the tow truck operator. Gillian pulled over to the side of the road but stayed in the car. She grabbed her digital camera and adjusted the zoom to the 800mm lens. Two paramedics rolled a gurney up the embankment. They stopped at the back door of the ambulance as the sheriff approached. One of them lifted the white sheet so he could see. Gillian pulled off a shot. The victim appeared to be a middle-aged man, early forties, covered in dried blood, seaweed and gnats.

"Cause of death?" the sheriff asked.

"Well, I suspect this five inch slit across his throat had something to do with it."

The sheriff paid him no mind. *Everybody's got*

an attitude today, he muttered to himself. He reached inside the victim's pocket and took out a wallet. A shiny metal badge glistened in the sunlight.

"Law enforcement," Gillian remarked out loud, as she snapped a few more. She glanced down at the camera's display screen to inspect the photos.

He was front and center before she knew it. "What do you think you're doing here?" Sam yelled at her. The split vein in his forehead had returned.

She rattled off a response without taking a breath. "I happened to be in the neighborhood-was that a police badge I saw you take out of that deadman's jacket?"

"Leave. Now. I have too much to do without you adding to it."

"It was, wasn't it? Who did he work for, Sam?"

"Gus," yelled the sheriff. "Please take Miss Gillian back to the station house and impound her car."

"All right. All right. I'll go." She threw the stick in reverse and backed away.

A few minutes later, back home, the utility truck was gone, and the postman had stopped by. Gillian threw the stack of mail on the kitchen table. Her head began to ache. She opened the freezer door and leaned inside. Relief. Somewhat. An ice pack would have to wait.

Amongst an array of computer hardware and peripherals, she downloaded the pictures to her laptop and stared at the victim's neck. She was lucky to get the shot. His skin looked gray with patches of caked, dried blood. Along the slit of his throat, the flesh was curled back and ragged. *What a way to die,* she thought. She scrolled through the photos until she came to a clear one of the shield. Not a local cop, but the FBI. What on earth was the FBI doing here? A name. She needed a name. She reached for the switch to the police band radio and turned on the unit. No chatter. Nothing. Sam was on to her, and knew she would be listening. She'd ask Lorelei later and went back to the kitchen.

Gillian flipped through the unopened mail. Catalogs, flyers, the phone bill and a small gray envelope addressed to her. She ripped it open. Inside was a handwritten note on Sol's letterhead. Her heart skipped a beat. The letter was postmarked the day before yesterday, and it read:

Dear Gillian,

It is difficult to put into words the peculiar aspects of the life I now leave behind. By now you know I have either left this beautiful island you call home, or have succumbed to a terrible fate. Either way, I am afraid our association may cause you harm, so I'm writing this to warn you to take heed. Strangers will come asking a lot of questions. Trust no-one! This is crucial. If things get out of hand, your security is the Tokyo Rose. You are like the daughter I never had, and I will treasure the time we spent together. Make a good life for yourself.

I will miss you, Vladimir Polinsky (Sol)

Gillian sat on a kitchen barstool, motionless,

staring at the letter, mulling over his warning. *Strangers?* This island was a haven for strangers. She carefully slid the note back into the envelope and placed it in her lap drawer. Her hands were shaking. She wished the throbbing in her head would go away.

Vladimir Polinsky. *Was that his real name or yet another alias*, she wondered. She needed to find his sailboat, the Tokyo Rose. Maybe he had stashed something onboard, and that's what the killer was looking for.

As she was about to fire off another email to Uncle Jack, a response to her first one came through. It read:

> *"I made a few inquiries on your behalf. Called in a few favors, so I hope this is worth it. Basically, there are some unhappy Russian mobsters looking for pink diamonds they lay claim to, as well as some missing plutonium. Other parties involved may include an Islamic cell with German Brazilian money connections, which of course, means Mossad is involved. For heaven's sake, Gillian, I hope you haven't gotten the family involved in something that will end up on some twenty-four hour cable news show."*

Gillian rolled her eyes. He worried too much about their precious family's reputation. At the risk of irritating him further, she shot off a one line email adding yet another name to her request: Vladimir Polinsky.

Next, it was onto the marina. The Tokyo Rose was docked in Slip 113. The hatch would probably be locked. She reached inside her bottom desk drawer and retrieved a small leather pouch. Inside, wrapped in an old piece of linen, were some specialty tools she'd not laid her hands on in quite some time. Not since her last bout with severe boredom. Diamonds. It was time to go find a cache of stolen blood diamonds. She shook her head in disgust, for she truly hated those freakin' things.

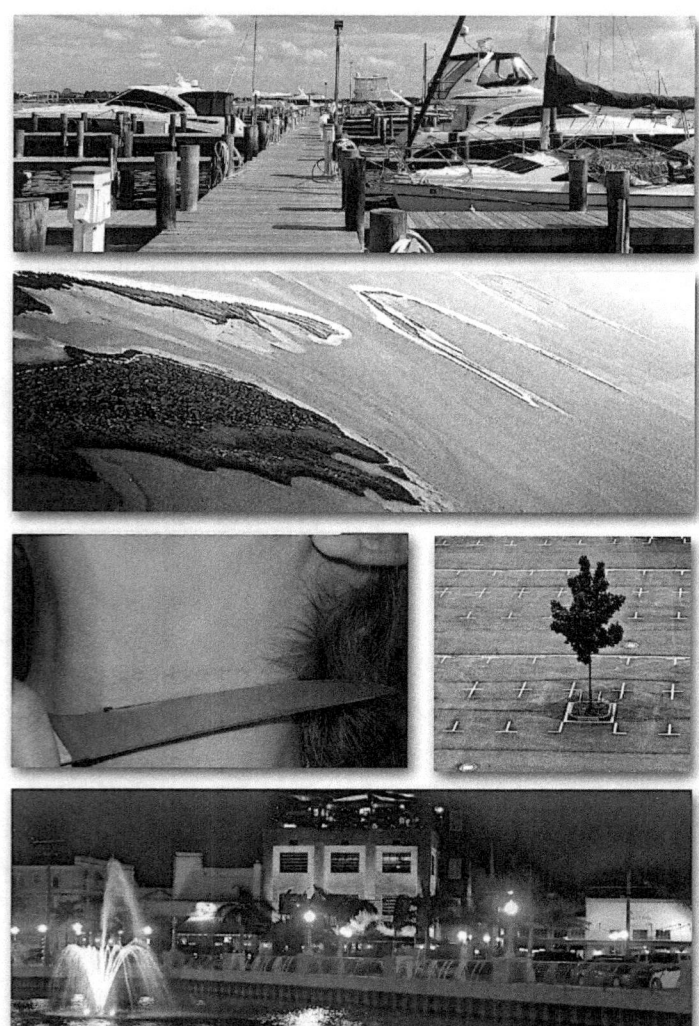

Chapter 6

The Boca Grande Marina was not particularly large, but what a sailor's delight. With deep channel waters surrounding the island, getting in and out was straightforward and unproblematic. The once legendary hideout for infamous pirate ships, now moored 50 foot yachts, massive catamarans, and intrepid sailboats. All arguably more yaw than the next.

Gillian parked her MG next to the Icehouse, then headed to the south pier; the section reserved for commercial fisherman and locals not into the yachting scene. The marina was located on the inland side of the island, which provided small barrier protection from the dangerous Gulf storms. The air was tainted with the smell of dead fish and marine wax: this morning's catch mixed with the laboring efforts of the local deck hands. Slip 113 was the location of Sol's 36 foot sailboat, the *Tokyo Rose*. A name purportedly inspired by a geisha, or so she was told.

As Gillian walked down the sun baked, wooden pier, she stopped by a brilliant yellow and red cigarette boat, named *'Ain't Misbehavin.'* She tugged twice on the line which secured it to the piling. It was her boat, and the name, her modus operandi, a misnomer if you asked some. A 55 footer with twin 500 horse Mercs. An expensive way to get to Key West in a hurry.

Gillian peered eagerly to the end of the pier. Empty. Sol's sailboat was gone. Gillian rubbed her forehead. Her so-called *'insurance'* was nowhere in sight.

"Sol, Sol, Sol," she moaned in frustration. "What is going on?" She stood on the pier for a moment, shook her head, then retreated back to the office. The dock master, Henry James, was an old friend of her family's. A salty dog, with a faint Irish accent.

"Good Morning, Miss Gillian. How ye be today?"

Gillian smiled bleakly. "Morning, Henry. How's the tournament going?"

"Busy, as you might expect. What can I do for you, lassie?"

"I'm looking for Mr. Crawford's sail boat, the Tokyo Rose. She's not in her usual slip. I was hoping to retrieve my sunglasses. I left them in the hull our last time out."

"Umm ... let me see," he said attentively. "Oh, yes. Mr. Crawford took her out three or four days ago. He left his car here overnight, which is odd. He's not one to usually sleep on board. The next day when I opened up shop, his car and boat were both gone. I guess he came back late in the evening and got his sedan. Can't say what happened to his boat though."

"Did he say where he was going?"

"Well, you know how he is, doesn't talk much. He did buy some navigational charts before he left, though."

"Really, what of, Henry?"

"Three actually. Useppa Island, Sanibel, and the Dry Tortugas."

"Did he mention any travel plans?"

"No. No, he didn't. Is everything all right?"

"Oh ... yeah. Everything's fine, Henry," she said, sounding somewhat preoccupied. She patted his forearm affectionately and added, "You know me, a curious sort. I best let you get back to work. I remember how crazy things can get when a big tournament is in play. Thanks. I'll catch up with you later."

Gillian walked back to her car and tried to sort things out. Sol must of moved his sailboat to another marina close by, otherwise, he wouldn't have gotten back by morning to move his car before Henry arrived. And fisherman like Henry were always up early. Super early. Gillian opened the glove compartment and studied an area map. Those navigational charts were all for locations south of Gasparilla Island.

Her fingers moved slowly down the map's coastline. A handful of marinas came to mind: Bokeelia; the Charlotte Docks; Fisherman's Wharf; and the Fort Myers Yacht Basin.

Gillian spent the rest of the afternoon in and out of every marina she knew between Boca Grande and Fort Myers. By 5:30 p.m. she pulled into downtown Fort Myers. It had been years since she'd visited this particular marina. With the last two expansion projects, the place had doubled in size. Hundreds of boats, with a myriad of prices, shapes and sizes. Million dollar yachts to 20 foot pontoons. The boardwalk, a mix of quirky little eating establishments, and hi-rise condominiums, was jam-packed with Yankees, who stayed in Southwest Florida from October to Easter.

Gillian realized there was precious little daylight

left to inspect the entire marina, so she went straight to the office, and asked to speak to the dock master.

Captain Archie Miller, had the night shift, and was delighted to assist. It didn't hurt when Gillian dropped her car keys in front of him, and had to retrieve them in her short, white skirt. His answer was music to her ears. Mr. Crawford had indeed rented a slip, just a few days ago. Paid for a month's rental in cash. Slip 227, down the east side pier and to the left.

The marina was alive with flickering lights, hanging from railings, masts and upper bridges. It was a moveable feast with the savory smell of grilled seafood, charcoal, and plenty of beer. The sounds of reggae and jazz from the neighboring river-walk provided musical ambiance, while the sunset left the sky with a beautiful mix of purple, pink and coral hues, speckled with a few early stars.

Gillian followed the descending slip numbers painted in black, to yet another empty birth: Slip 227. "Crap," she uttered out loud. "Now what do I do?" Nailed to the slip piling was a dilapidated wooden picture frame, with nothing in it. *Peculiar accent,* she thought. Gillian glanced around. All three neighbors, a 46 foot Sea Ray, an 80 foot Hatteras, and a 40 foot catamaran, were closed up for the evening. No help making inquiries tonight. Frustrated, she turned around and headed for her car.

As she made her way down the city sidewalk, about a hundred yards from her MG, Gillian heard the sound of footsteps approaching from behind. Hard soles on pavement. She stopped and turned around. Nothing. The day had left her nerves a little raw. She was hungry and tired, and could use a stiff drink.

As she fumbled with her keys and unlocked the car door, someone grabbed her from behind. He was strong and overpowering. The usual defense tactics were useless. One hand reached over her mouth, the other around her waist. Gillian stopped her struggle and became extremely still. A blade flipped open and skimmed her neck. She could smell the rich, distinct scent of musk.

"Shhh," he began in a low pitched voice. "We know who you are, and we know where you live. Stop looking for the Tokyo Rose, or else you'll end up like your friend. Are we clear?" He reached up and caressed the side of her face, then slowly ran his fingers through her silky, brown hair. Gillian shook in revulsion. She felt the sharp edge of the blade at the base of her throat.

"I'd hate for such a beautiful woman like yourself to end up that way." He lowered his voice and whispered in her ear. "Although I'm sure I could make my next visit quite pleasurable."

Gillian stiffened and held her breath. Slowly he ran his fingers down the front of her blouse and fondled her breast. She could feel his hot breath against her cheek. A whimper slipped through her lips. Suddenly he threw her hard against the car, then down on the pavement. Her head hit the road, and she blacked out. She never got a look at him.

When Gillian came to, she reached for the door handle, and pulled herself up. He was gone. She brushed the road debris off her face and grimaced.

There were several scrapes on her forehead, and her head was pounding. Her mind was screaming, *get out of here!* Gillian scoured the pavement looking for her keys. Nothing. She peered under the car. Still nothing. They were gone.

Inside the MG, she reached under the dash and yanked out a set of multicolored wires. After a few taps together of the exposed ends, she got a spark and the engine turned over. Hadley's training, God bless him. She threw the gearshift into first and peeled out.

As she squealed around the northbound ramp to the interstate, a stray tear ran down her red cheek. Her heart was still racing. She was lucky. She was stupid. And now she was angry. Gillian mashed down on the clutch and slammed the stick into fourth. The speedometer needle read 90 and was quivering. The engine was getting hot.

How on earth did they find me, she wondered? She'd been careful. She watched for a tail. It didn't make sense. That's when she slammed on the brakes, downshifted and fishtailed to a halt. Gillian grabbed a flashlight out of the glove compartment and got out. Slowly and methodically she walked around the car, shining the bright light along the outside. Bingo. She found it. A smeared handprint on the back fender. The road dust had acted as fingerprint powder, exposing it. She got down on her hands and knees and peered underneath. There it was. A small orange box with a transmitter stuck to the fuel tank. A GPS tracking device. She yanked off the contraption.

Once back in her car, she headed north, staying

true to what they would assume to be her local route home. No hint that she had found their device. She would head to the hotel, have Hadley take a look, then decide what to do from there.

The Interstate between Fort Myers and Port Charlotte, at night, was lightly traveled, making for a dark, monotonous highway. A few clouds had moved in; not many stars. As she crossed the county line and went over a hill, her radar detector went off. Too late. He had her. The blue lights came on within seconds. She slowed down, signaled and exited onto the side of the road.

"Good evening, Miss. Do you know why I stopped you?"

Gillian just smiled and bit her tongue.

"License and registration, please." He was a State Trooper, middle aged, a little worn around the edges, with a monotone voice.

He glanced at her license. "Where are you headed, Miss Crawford?"

"I've been in Fort Myers on business, and now I'm headed home." On any other night, she would have turned on the charm to try and beat the citation, but this evening, her voice was still shaky from her attack, and he already pegged her guilty of something.

"I need for you to step out of the car, please."

The officer proceeded to give Gillian the standard roadside sobriety test: walk the line, touch your nose. Annoyed, Gillian rolled her eyes but passed without incident.

"Did you have any problems in Fort Myers this evening?" He noticed the scratches on her face.

By this time, Gillian was agitated and sighed. "No sir, why?"

"The sheriff in Boca Grande called in your vehicle description. He asked if we'd keep an eye out for you."

"Oh he did, did he." She was pissed. "I'm sure you have more important things to do," she glanced at his name tag, "Officer Keaton. He shouldn't have troubled you."

The officer ripped a ticket off his pad and handed it to her. He sensed the tension in her voice. The sheriff had given him the heads up on Miss Crawford: fierce temper, but easy on the eyes.

"I suggest you take it easy from here on out. Have a safe evening." To make matters worse, he followed her all the way up the interstate until the beach cut off.

By this time, Gillian was seeing red.

Chapter 7

It was nearly nine o'clock by the time Gillian turned off the intercostal highway, onto the two lane road back home. The pain in her head was unbearable. For the person who seemed to live a charmed life, migraines were her suffering lot. She had a litany of triggers; the sheriff being one of them.

"Life is tough, so buck up," her Uncle Jack told her after the death of her parents. He was not the nurturing type. So she did; alone, and without complaint. At social gatherings, she would sometimes disappear without explanation. People often pegged her as eccentric, not knowing otherwise. Only a select few knew of her malady. They were told to mind their own business. Sam and Hadley being amongst them. Those two also knew of Gillian's choice of pain management and turned a blind eye.

The Crawford family rose garden had been featured in a dozen horticultural magazines over the last twenty years; three hundred plus specimens of antiques, hybrids and climbers. A knot garden layout, with cobblestone paths. Gillian employed two grounds keepers to manage the flowers, as well as the surrounding lawns. She rarely interacted, except to pay their invoices for services rendered, and their much appreciated discretion.

Nestled deep within the mix of dark pink Zephirine Drouhin roses, were several innocuous Cannabis Salvia that provided complimentary aesthetic appeal. The plants were strategically placed inside a circle of the meandering climbers. A deterrent for those not knowing their uniqueness of being thornless. Gillian made a beeline for the garden and checked the status of the buds: almost time to harvest. Perfect, since her supply was getting low.

Moments later, she unlatched the roof top opening to the old widow's walk and climbed out. The white railed platform surrounded the chimney and provided ready access in case of fire. Built around the turn of the 20th Century, it was also a part of the family's mariner ancestry.

Up top, the landing was uncluttered, often breezy, and provided an exceptional place to pace. The cool wind on her face was soothing. She laid down on the white chaise lounge, finished the joint and closed her eyes. At its worst, it was hard to lie still. Her feet would twist and turn while her hands would squeeze her temples, trying to shut down the pain. The nausea was hit or miss. As her head would pound, she would count the heart beats. For the next hour or so, everything would slow down. She traded pain relief for the vulnerability of being stoned, but that was okay. Traditional meds helped, but left her out of commission for a solid day. This was quicker, better, although there was the bothersome legality issue.

A short while later, Gillian plodded across her kitchen floor and splashed some cold water on her face. She felt better, not great, but was famished. Her refrigerator was empty. When she sat down at her desk to call the local pizza delivery, she realized the lap drawer was pulled askew. Sol's letter, which she had placed inside, was missing. Gillian rustled through the contents as she searched for the envelope. It was gone. Her mind was a bit foggy, but she was certain she had placed it there. Gillian quickly accessed the security system log from her laptop, and spotted two entries back to back. She pushed her chair aside, spun around and studied the room. Her throat tightened. She reached for her cell phone, punched in a memorized set of function keys and waved it in the air. The detection device homed right in on a bug. A clever enhancement from Hadley. Her hand reached for the landline handset and slowly unscrewed the mouthpiece. A little red listening device slipped out, dangling from a gray wire. She yanked on the bug and severed the connection.

"What the bloody hell are you doing here?" she cursed annoyingly. Her first inclination was to smash it to pieces. It creeped her out to think of someone entering her home, violating her space, spying on her. Gillian spun slowly around in her chair and flipped *the bird* to whoever was watching. Under her desk, she fumbled with a package secured by duct tape, and ripped it free. A .45 caliber Glock dropped into her hands. She checked the clip, stuffed the bug in her pocket and ran for the door.

Sam Mitchell lived three doors down from Gillian in a renovated cottage once owned by the church. A parsonage, from days gone by, dwarfed on both sides by private estates the size of Gillian's, making it barely noticeable as a place of residence.

Gillian sped down his driveway. The gun was out in the open on the passenger's seat. She had barely decided what to say when a flood light came on, and the front door opened. "Damn motion detector," she mumbled to herself.

Sam stood in the doorway looking puzzled. He spotted the gun but said nothing. He was still dripping wet from the shower, donned only in a black towel. There was an awkward moment between them as Gillian enjoyed the view. Eye candy. If only he came with a muzzle.

Sam noticed her pupils and reached up to touch her cheek. "Are you all right?"

Gillian ducked under his arm and invited herself in. "I'm starving. Do you have anything to eat?" She opened his refrigerator and reached for some strawberries. As she stood at the door checking the contents, Sam walked up behind her. Close. Rousingly close. He smelled delicious. Gillian paused for a second and closed her eyes.

"How bad was it?" he asked as he turned her around.

She glanced up at him and smiled bleakly, not answering.

"Those scrapes along your forehead. You want to tell me what happened?" His hands reached up and smoothed her hair back.

She fibbed. "I tripped going up the circular steps to the widow's walk."

"Uh-huh. Sure you did." He could tell that was a lie. Ever since she had returned from abroad, her demeanor was guarded and enigmatic. Not at all like she used to be.

"Don't worry about it." She cleared her throat and changed her mind. She would deal with the break-in herself. "So, the reason I dropped by was to tell you I'm moving into Uncle Jack's suite at the hotel for a few days. I'm having the house fumigated. Found some nasty bugs. Just in case you were looking for me."

"All right. Duly noted." That was lame, he thought. The truth would come out later.

"Thanks for the police escort. Office Keaton, I believe." She glared at Sam, expecting him to fumble an apology.

"Just be thankful you weren't stoned when he pulled you over," he replied, matter-of-factly.

She started to rip him a reply, but he covered her mouth with his hand. He studied her face, trying to get a read on what she was up to. So gorgeous, he thought. If only he could duct tape her mouth.

Sam spun her around and led her to the doorway. "You damn well better take care of that gun. Go raid Hadley's kitchen, then get some rest. I'll talk to you in the morning. That is, if you see morning." He smacked her on the butt and shut the door.

GILLIAN, TRAVELING LIGHT, silently made her way across the polished, marble floor of the Boca Grande Hotel. With no events scheduled this evening, the resort was particularly quiet. The late night desk clerk, a college kid by the name of Trevor, was glued to a webcast of Jeopardy. He didn't hear her approach.

"Famous Quotations for 200, please."

There was a pause for the slide.

"This public figure once said, 'great minds discuss ideas; average minds discuss events; small minds discuss people.'"

"Who was Eleanor Roosevelt," Gillian answered out loud as she arrived at the front desk.

The night clerk jumped in surprise. "Uh, good evening, Miss Crawford. Sorry. I didn't hear you walk in."

"You know this show's addictive."

He nodded as they both tuned in for the next question.

"70's Bestsellers for 300, please."

Again the slide turned.

"This book depicts a 17 day journey exploring the Metaphysics of Quality."

"What is Zen and the Art of Motorcycle Maintenance," Gillian answered at the same time as the contestant. She looked down at the desk clerk and smiled. "Guess you missed that day in school, huh?"

"I suppose," he replied, embarrassed she was intellectually whipping his butt. "What can I do for you this evening, ma'am?"

"I'm going to be staying in my uncle's suite for a few days, so could I get a key? Also, do you know if Hadley is still around?"

He glanced at the clock on the wall. "He usually leaves about this time, but I haven't seen him walk out yet. Would you like me to phone the kitchen?"

"No, I'll swing by in a minute. Thank you, Trevor. Good luck with your game."

Gillian knocked on the stainless steel door of the hotel's kitchen but did not wait for a reply.

Hadley was pouring himself a cup of coffee and yelled without looking, "Sorry, we're closed."

"Too bad 'cause I'm starving."

Hadley glanced up and spotted her. One look at her eyes explained it all.

"Have the munchies?"

"Yes, I'm starving. Whataya have?"

"Well, let's see. We have some roasted beef tenderloin with wild mushrooms, foie gras, garlic mashed potatoes with black truffle sauce, or a light sautéed snapper filet with white wine saffron sauce and artichoke filled piquillo peppers. Take your pick."

Gillian grabbed two buffet size dinner plates to satisfy her appetite.

"You want to tell me what you did to your forehead?"

"I had a personal warning delivered to me in Fort Myers, at the Yacht Basin."

"What exactly are you saying?" he asked with grave concern. Hadley made a promise to Jonathan Alistair Cromwell years ago to watch Gillian's back, before and after they left their employer. An arrangement that had seen them through some dodgy situations in the past five years.

Gillian proceeded to fill him in on the day's events: Sol's murder; Sol's letter; Sol's missing boat; a dead FBI agent; the mugging at the marina; the planted GPS tracking device, and the break in at her house. All the while, devouring both plates of food.

"And to think all I managed to do today was slave over a hot stove." They both chuckled. "What can I do to help?"

"Two things, actually. First, I need my house swept for any remaining bugs. That jacked up phone you gave me, found a listening device in the landline handset." She reached into her pocket and tossed both the tracking device and the little red jewel on the prep table. "Second, I was hoping you could plant some of your own in the centerpieces you set out at breakfast. I'm interested in any Russian dialog you might pick up."

"I can handle that. Are you staying here tonight?"

"Yes. Uncle Jack's suite." Gillian tried to stifle a yawn.

"Good. Feeling better now?"

"Much. Everything was delicious, as usual."

"Oh, by the way, thanks for those mid-court playoff tickets. How did you manage that?'

She just smiled and shrugged her shoulders.

"Shall I walk you up?"

"No, I've intruded enough. I'll be fine. Thanks, though. I'll drop by in the morning."

Gillian grabbed the key and headed for the elevator. A moment later she entered the mahogany lift and pushed the brass button for the third floor. The doors closed slowly. The smell that greeted her was overwhelming: musk. A chill ran down her spine.

She reached into her jacket pocket for the Glock. The elevator stopped on the third floor. The doors opened, and she carefully peaked around the corner. The hallway was empty. Gillian made a dash for her uncle's suite at the far end. The elevator sounded off, and the doors closed.

Gillian laid her gun on the night stand and turned down the bed. Uncle Jack, being a full blown security freak, had a motion detection system installed in a suite he never stayed in. Gillian went over to the fingerprint scanner and logged in. Sleep was a moment away.

As she turned off the remaining lights and double checked the locks, an envelope appeared under the door. She peered through the peephole, but there was no one in sight. Gillian tore open the envelope. The note read:

'If you're interested in who killed Solomon Crawford, I'll be the high bidder on Lot #11 tomorrow night at the art auction'.

It was signed, *Max Taylor*.

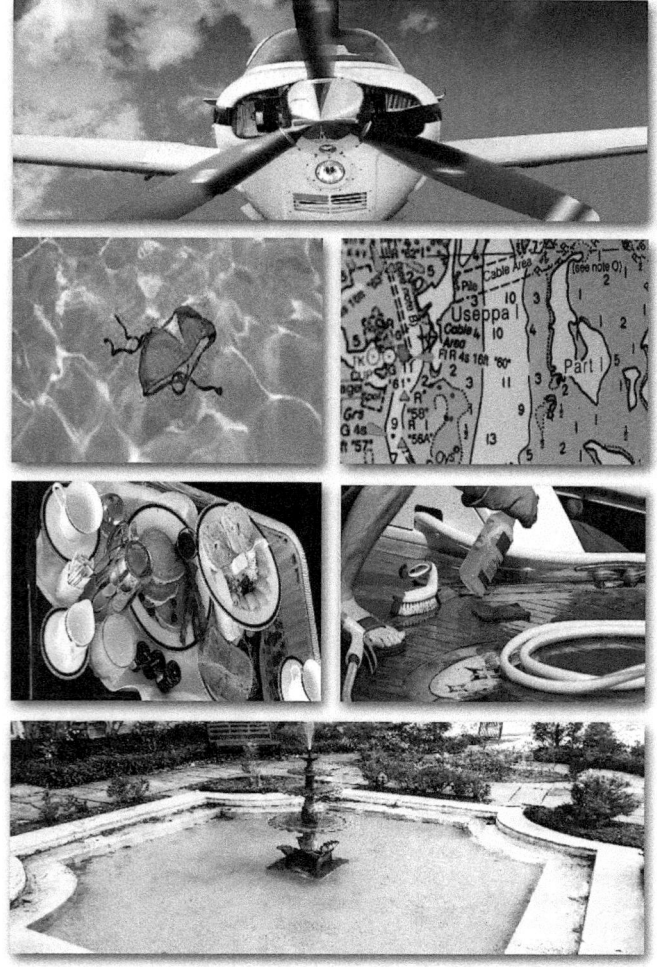

Chapter 8

"**R**oom Service," a young member of the hotel staff announced outside Room 309. It was eight o'clock in the morning.

Roused from a drug laden sleep, Gillian walked splay-footed to the door, fumbled with the chain and disarmed the system. The waiter, with a garment bag flung over his shoulder, wheeled the breakfast table into the center of the suite without incident.

Gillian made a sprint for the bathroom, splashed some water on her face, and smoothed down her hair. She leaned over the counter, gazed into the mirror and cringed. The young waiter, waiting around the corner, cleared his throat.

"Good Morning, Miss Crawford," he greeted her with an energetic voice. She hated energetic this early in the morning. "I took the liberty of hanging a garment bag in your front closet. It arrived here this morning. Also, the chef wanted me to give you this." He reached out and handed her a sealed envelope, hotel stationary, pale gray parchment, then proceeded to pour her a cup of strong coffee, boss's orders.

Gillian glanced up from the letter and realized he was waiting for a reply. The smile from his brilliant white teeth gleamed in contrast to his tanned face and shiny black hair. *His ponytail was charming*, she mused, *bet the young girls loved that*. She fumbled through her wallet and handed him a ten.

Gillian feigned a smile. He understood. She looked like a train wreck, but he never let on.

"Thank you," glancing at his name tag, "Enrique. Tell your boss I'll stop by later."

"Yes, ma'am, I will. And thank you." He shoved the bill into his pocket, smiled a little longer than decorum would dictate, then backed out of the doorway.

Nothing coy about him, she shook her head.

Gillian ripped open the envelope and read the note:

> *"The bug man will be at your home around ten. New centerpieces were set out this morning. Have you written your welcome speech for the art auction tonight? Busy day. TTYL"*

The art auction was Uncle Jack's annual black tie soiree, to benefit whatever his philanthropic cause of the month was. Gillian couldn't keep up. His staff handled the details, but she, representing the family, had to get up and say a few welcoming words. He remained a recluse.

Between the art auction and the fishing tournament, the hotel was booked. Lots of strangers, each with their own agenda. *Wonderful,* she thought. The question was how to weed out the regulars from the fray. She paced the floor while eating a warm bagel, topped with salmon and cream cheese. Tasty. Hadley had made a good choice.

Gillian sat down at the desk, booted up Uncle Jack's laptop, which he never used, and entered a few back door key commands to hack into the hotel's reservation database. She heard a mentoring voice inside her head, reminding her to not leave verifiable footprints.

The hotel had one hundred thirty rooms, including suites. Seventy percent had been here before. Thirty five rooms were first time guests; eleven being single occupant males. Some help, but not much, all with Anglo-Saxon Protestant surnames. *Naturally,* she grumbled and rolled her awakening green eyes. Gillian printed off a list of first timers and placed it in her wallet. Three cups of coffee later, she was on her way downstairs to visit Hadley.

Gillian peeked inside the kitchen a few moments later. It was mid-morning, between the breakfast and lunch shifts. Usually Hadley would be outside bumming a smoke. But not today. With a black tie function this evening, Hadley had his full staff at work. The place was noisy and chaotic, with dishes falling, grease flames bursting, tempers flaring. The sous chef was having-it-out with a produce vendor. Hadley glanced up from a workstation of grilled seafood tapas and duck liver canapés and shook his head. Not a good time. She formed the word *'sorry'* with her lips and exited through the metal door.

THE SUN WAS directly overhead when the marina hand finished topping off the tanks to Gillian's cigarette boat. He cast a cool, but guarded glance up and down the pier, before moving on.

Gillian pulled into the marina parking lot shortly thereafter, still on the hunt for the Tokyo Rose. Her plan was to visit some out-of-the-way spots not accessible by motor vehicle. The trouble being, the more secluded the location, the more tight lipped the residents tended to be. They paid a lot of money to be left alone.

Gillian's speed boat zig-zagged through the channel markers on the way out to Boca Grande Pass. The strong current, wind and deep water made for a rough passage. Never a place for squeamish stomachs. The boat slammed hard into the white caps, spraying salt water on her face and arms. It was too uncomfortable to sit. She eased up on the throttle. Gillian recognized several of the local sea captains out on charters as their clients unloaded their wallets in hopes of hooking *'the big one.'* As they trolled by, fine-tuning the drag on their reels, she gave the customary hand wave to total strangers, which on land would seldom occur.

Once through the Pass, Gillian headed over to the calmer waters behind a barrier key, in route to her first stop: Useppa. The island had its own clandestine history; the hideaway for the famous pirate Jose Gasper, and the training ground of Cuban exiles for the Bay of Pig Operation in the Sixties. A Kennedy Administration/CIA nightmare. What a difference fifty plus years made. Now the island was back to its former glory, as in the early 1900's when Barron Collier, the once largest landowner in the state of Florida, had a vested interest. Useppa had a very private, highly elite, sporting club back in the day. Now it was just plain private.

Gillian was still several minutes away when suddenly the engines of the '*Ain't Misbehavin'* began to chug. She pulled back on the throttle. The twin engines sputtered, backfired, then stopped. Gillian threw the gearshift into neutral and turned the key.

"Come on, come on," she yelled to the silent engines. Nothing. Gillian flipped the transmit switch to the two-way radio. That was dead too. "Bloody Hell!" she cursed, looking out over the horizon. No boats on this side of the island. She placed her hands akimbo, perturbed. She had no time for this. There were places to go, people to see. The orange distress flag went up, the anchor went down, and the air-horn screamed. There was nothing more to do now, but wait.

Gillian grabbed a beach towel and seat cushion, then headed to the bow of the boat. The weather was sunny and hot. Beads of sweat rolled down the curves of her chest. She unscrewed the cap from an iced down bottle of sparkling water and placed the cold container against her cheek. Boat trouble made her blood boil. She took off her t-shirt, untied her bikini's strap and laid down up front. An hour or so passed. Gillian dozed off to sleep.

The sound of a single prop airplane jolted her awake. She sat up and scoured the sky, shielding her eyes from the sun. The aircraft was directly south and descending fast. Gillian jumped up and down, waving the bright blue towel in her hands. The pilot responded, tipping the plane's wings. *What a relief,* she thought. Now that she had been located, rescue would be on the way. She reached down, gathered her shirt, then glanced up again at the plane. Something was wrong. It continued its descent, taking aim now like a kamikaze pilot. *Surely he would pull up,* she reasoned. What was he doing? In less than five seconds, he would ram her boat.

Gillian rushed to the stern. As her feet bounced

off the back end, she dove out and away. On impact, her bikini top came off. The salt water stung her eyes as she swam straight down to escape the blast. Her chest was screaming for air. Nothing happened. No explosion. She struggled to make out the outline of her boat. Slowly, Gillian drifted to the surface but stayed clear of the vessel. The plane was gone, flying north towards the mainland. She rubbed her eyes trying to focus. The N Registration number was a blur.

A 58 foot sedan bridge blew its horn, cruising to her rescue. Gillian, treading water, waved her arms and swam towards the yacht. She recognized the captain and first mate: Carmine and Vinnie, complete with Hawaiian shirts, tats, and muscles to spare.

The attractive one with a flat nose spoke first. "Yo, restaurant lady, you okay? We watched that plane take a nose dive, and decided to head over to this side of the island. You need some help?"

"Well yes, actually. I seem to have lost a piece of my bathing suit."

He broke out in a smile. "Can't help you with that."

With one effortless swoop, the two men lifted her out of the water, up on deck, and handed her a towel and dry t-shirt. Good thing Gillian wasn't modest.

"Won't this be a memorable first impression." She smiled and extended her hand.

"Hey, how you doin? I'm Pauly, this is Renzo, Glad to be of service. Here have a seat." Renzo nodded his head but remained silent. Clearly he did not enjoy the gift of gab.

"Gillian Crawford. Pleased to meet you. I can't thank you enough for coming to my rescue. First my boat engines die, second that plane tried to ram me, then my bathing suit malfunctions." She shook her head, still in disbelief.

"Have you radioed in for a tow?"

"No, that's another thing. Now my radio is on the fritz."

"Geeze, lady. Someone trying to tell you something?"

"My thoughts exactly."

"Renzo," Pauly said, "call the marina, and tell them we need a tow."

Renzo left the deck and went to the upper helm. Gillian patted herself dry but began to shiver. The apprehension she felt was obvious. Out in the middle of nowhere, with two complete strangers who happened to be in the vicinity when she was nearly mowed down by a plane. *What were the chances,* she wondered.

"You look like you could use a drink. Whataya like? We gotta full bar."

"Water's fine. Thank you."

"Oh, come on. I make a very dry martini."

Gillian hesitated, then agreed. He was extremely attentive, whether by design or not. At this point, her choices were clearly limited. Make the most of the situation, she decided, and try to be cordial.

"Nice boat," she began.

"Yours too."

"Except when she breaks down."

"Yeah, well this is my Uncle Tony's. He let Renzo and me use her this week to do some fishin."

"Oh, so you're here for the tournament?"

'Nah, let's just say we needed to get away for a while. You know how it is."

Gillian smiled. In other words, Pauly and Renzo were wise guys and needed to lay low until the heat died down. Well at least they weren't Russian Mobsters or Jihad Muslims. Gillian sipped her drink and relaxed a little more. When she woke up this morning, she never guessed she'd befriend the Italian Mafia today, and seek refuge in their company. All things considered, this pathetic outing might turn out to her advantage, for the Mafioso clearly hated the Russian Mafia. Renzo remained AWOL for the next half hour while Pauly and Gillian made small talk, waiting for the tow-barge to arrive.

"So what brings you here, vacation?" he asked.

"No. I live here. Born and raised." Gillian shrugged her shoulders as if she had no excuse to offer.

"I didn't think there were many of youz guys still around. Seems like a bunch of damn Yankees to me."

"A handful of families remain with ties to the original settlers."

"Settlers," he chuckled as he refilled her glass. "You mean pirates, don't ya?" he added. His shiny, black eyes were warm, yet dangerous.

"Brushing up on the local history, I see."

"Well, when the sidewalks roll up at ten, you've gotta find something to do."

"My great-great-grandfather was the first mate of Jose Gasper. Hence, Gasparilla Island."

He nodded that he got it.

"He fell in love with the island and decided to

settle down. Went into the phosphorous business.
Became legit. Married well. End of story."

"Bet you have some interesting family skeletons
in your closet," he said.

"Probably like your Palermo family closet," she
replied back, straight faced.

They each looked expressionless at one another
before bursting into laughter.

"Here's to closets," he said and clicked his glass
with hers.

"Absolutely. It's who we are," she added.

"You've got that right." He poured her another.

Highly unusual ally to have at the moment,
Gillian thought.   The   association   might   prove
valuable. Extremely valuable.

"So this treasure hunting stuff I hear about. Any
truth to it?"

"Some," she responded, turning serious. "The
stories you read in those paperback books are a little
over the top. Helps the tourist trade, though. Seems
like each time a hurricane blows through, the storm
stirs up the ocean floor moving the wrecks around.
How the process works is, the State leases you a
quadrant and takes a percentage of whatever you
salvage.   Some grad students discovered a few
Spanish medallions right outside the Pass about forty
feet down after Hurricane Charlie came through a
while back. That brought a slew of fortune hunters in
for the season, which is good for business."

"I bet."

"If you're interested, I can point you in the right
direction. It's the least I can do since you pulled me
out of the drink."

"Nah, we're more the above-the-water kind of guys."

"Well, how about some fishing holes, only the locals know of?"

Renzo, in earshot of the conversation, arrived with map in hand. Gillian showed him several spots that were popular for redfish and tarpon. He seemed generally appreciative.

"So, what brings you to the hotel since you live here."

"I hate to cook, and the hotel's chef is a friend of mine."

Notwithstanding their particular line of work, they were interesting fellas. Gillian endured the arduous sexual glances of Pauly while sipping a ready supply of martinis. Renzo disappeared again, manning the helm.

When they finally arrived back on shore, Gillian kissed them both on the cheek, thanked them profusely for rescuing her, then teetered to her car. She was in serious need of some coffee. Pulling the printout from her wallet, she crossed Paul Smith and Reynold Johnson off the list. Down to nine.

Twice in the last twenty-four hours she had skirted death. It was a surreal feeling, difficult to get her head around. Gillian took a deep breath and started her car. As if by fate, her cell phone rang. The caller ID read: FFF. It was a call she had to take.

Father Francis Flannigan, the local priest from St. Michael's had an uncanny way of contacting her when she least wanted to talk. The difference between Father Francis, as she referred to him, and Uncle Jack's favors were, he always said, *'thank you.'*

"Gillian, did I catch you at a bad time?"

"No, Father, what's up?"

"Would you mind stopping by before the fundraiser this evening?"

"How about right now?"

"Yes, that would be perfect."

"Alrighty. I'll see you in a few."

ST. MICHAEL'S WAS located across the street from Sam Mitchell's house. The parish was small. A courtyard and founders cemetery separated the church from Father Flannigan's living quarters. It was a compound setting, surrounded by an eight foot brick wall. Gillian found him sitting on a wooden stool in the courtyard, with an easel, doing paint by numbers. Late forties, a little gray around the edges, loved to play soccer with the kids. His eyes sparkled all the time. It was well with his soul.

"Sistine Chapel, is it?"

"It's supposed to be, but I'm having my doubts."

"Patience, Father. It's a virtue." Gillian chuckled and patted him on the back.

"Glad you paid attention. I believe that was the topic of my sermon three weeks ago. Haven't seen you lately."

Gillian's guilt meter took a bounce. They had a pro-bono relationship for the *greater good*. He helped her with all matters pertaining to her soul; she helped him with unorthodox matters that needed tweaking. Many a parishioner benefited from Gillian's special way of fixing things. They never knew she was a good soldier, a crusader for those in need.

"Remember, my dear, it is Salvation that will get you into Heaven, not deeds. Deeds are awarded crowns when you get there. I pray you seek His guidance in everything you do, and thank Him for saving your soul. For He is the way, the truth and the light. No man cometh unto the Father, but by Him." It was a homely he often reiterated to her and to the members of the parish. He continued.

"I know you have a lot on your plate right now, but I wanted to visit with you for a moment. I have something for you." He reached into his pants pocket and took out a business card. "This was given to me by Solomon. I did not know it would be his last confession. He asked me to pass it on to you." Father Flannigan handed her the card.

Gillian glanced down at the name: Simon Cantore. Exports. Naples, Florida. On the back side were nautical coordinates only a local would recognize: 26.66N, 82.21W. It was Useppa Island.

"I will pray for travel mercies, Gillian. Come by and see me when you get back. Let us also pray the art auction is a remarkable success tonight. The children are in need of a new orphanage."

"Yes, Father. We should do that. By the way, what time is it?"

He looked at his watch. "Four o'clock."

"Time for me to go. Looks like you've got a job, getting all that paint off your hands."

"Latex, dear. It scrubs right off."

Chapter 9

Gillian entered the ballroom of the Boca Grande Hotel at ten minutes to seven. She wore a dark gray, satin cocktail dress, tapered, with beaded spaghetti straps. The selection was a perfect match for her toned, tanned body, killer legs, and smoldering eyes. She was ready to play the role of Jonathan Alistair Cromwell's gracious, attentive host. A night for beautiful people, in beautiful surroundings, with not-so-beautiful artwork.

At one end of the ballroom with its crystal chandeliers and gilded walls, was a podium, the settlement/payment table and rows of chairs. The other end was a mingling spot, where white jacketed waiters pushed Hadley's scrumptious hors d'oeuvres and magnums of champagne to the arriving guests.

Gillian threw back a half glass of courage and headed to the podium. She tapped the live microphone several times to gain attention, then cleared her throat.

"Good evening. On behalf of the Jonathan Alistair Cromwell Charitable Trust, I am Gillian Crawford, and I would like to welcome you this evening to our annual art auction. With the help of your generous bidding tonight, the local, and I might add, extremely crowded, orphanage will finally break ground on a much needed new home. So please, enjoy these delectable provisions with your cocktails. We will begin in half an hour. Thank you again, and have a wonderful evening. Cheers."

Gillian spotted Hadley at the side door. He toasted her with a champagne glass, nodded his head, and mouthed the words *'well done.'* He slipped away right after, for he was still on the clock.

Gillian scoured the attendees looking for a familiar face. She had thirty minutes to work the room. Before she could decide where to start, a guest was upon her. The androgynous secretary dressed in a frumpy black tuxedo was fully engaged and in her face.

"I wasn't sure the auction would take place this evening, given that recent press conference. And that scrape on your forehead does look fresh."

Gillian moved a half step back and responded with a straight face. "Sorry?"

"Helen Crenshaw, assistant to Mr. Dennis Witherspoon, Suite 203. Wonderful to meet you." The introduction was direct, the handshake too firm, her voice, a low register reserved for twenty year tobacco addicts with a fondness for Jack.

Before Gillian could formulate a response, she continued. "Like I said, I wasn't sure about the auction this evening. Crawford, huh? You related to the murdered victim?" It was an old trick, use abruptness to catch one off guard.

Gillian's defenses ratcheted up. In a sweet, magnolia voice, feigned with small mindedness she replied, "No, ma'am. The same last name is just a coincident. I understand Crawford was an alias, though." She leaned towards her and lowered her voice. "Rumor has it he was connected with the Russian Mafia. Can you imagine? Right here in our quaint little town. Those despicable foreigners." Her words were the perfect mix of gossip mongering and clueless society intellect. Gillian studied her body language; curious, waiting for the slightest reaction.

Even with the heavy pancake makeup, Gillian spotted the emerging vein in Miss Crenshaw's forehead. She had struck a nerve and shut her up. Up close, she was even more masculine than she originally noted. Her attempt at provoking a flattering look via makeup had failed. Mrs. Witherspoon, if indeed she did exist, had nothing to worry about.

"Do you collect art, Miss Crenshaw?"

"No. I'm here strictly for Mr. Witherspoon. He had a look at the auction catalog and was interested in a few pieces."

"I don't believe I've met him. Would you be so kind?" Gillian's eyes scaled the room, waiting for her to point him out.

"He's not joining us this evening. Still up in his suite, convalescing."

"Oh, that's too bad. I'll have the chef send up a tray of his delicious canapés."

"That won't be necessary. He's on a strict diet. Doctor's orders. Complete bed rest."

"I'm so sorry to hear that. Please give him my condolences." Gillian's hesitation was awkward. "If you'll excuse me. I need to check in with the auctioneer. By the way, I understand Lot 11 contains a painting of some merit. Good luck with your bidding, Miss Crenshaw. I'll see you later."

Gillian headed to the center of the room to another group of guests. All of them, in fact, were familiar faces from the breakfast crowd. A surprising mix to be conversing: the Texan with his trophy wife, the elderly couple straight out of an English novel, their grandsons, the Islamic husband and burka clad wife, and corporate America, Dick and Jane.

The Texan, in a boisterous voice, magnified by a significant consumption of champagne, began the introductions. "Miss Crawford, I'm Cletus Wilcox, this is my wife, Katlyn, we're from Midland, Texas." Gillian shook their hands.

He continued. "This is Homid Patel and his wife, Nadra, from Washington, D.C. "

"Good Evening," Gillian said.

"And Tilla and Johann VanBuren from Albany, NY."

"Hello, glad to meet you."

"Their grandsons, Ralph and Rem," he added.

"My pleasure."

"And this is," he hesitated and extended his hand, as if in need of assistance. Dick and Jane, as Gillian had coined them stepped forward. Both again, impeccably dressed. He in a black silk suit, she in the perfect little-black dress.

"Brock Hansen, and my wife, Christine."

"Ah, yes," Gillian replied, shaking their extended hands. "Newlyweds. Congratulations."

"That's right. Thank you," he replied looking somewhat surprised.

"How did you know, are we that obvious," Christine asked, as her arm went around her husband's waist in an awkward show of emotion.

"Simple really. I was admiring your diamond ring earlier, and noticed you fidgeting with the setting."

The couple passed a quick glance at one another

as if to say, *'keep an eye on this one.'*

"A small ceremony last week," she divulged.

"We met at a trade show in Atlanta last July," he added.

"Those are always crazy, but well worth going," Gillian said. "I was in Atlanta last January. What a shame they stopped having them at the Mart, wouldn't you agree?"

"Yes, a real shame," Brock answered, turning attention to his drink.

Gillian smiled and turned to the other guests in the circle. Brock Hansen was full of crap. The Mart, in Atlanta, was still the premiere venue for trade shows.

Gillian focused her attention on the English novel couple. "VanBuren, as in the 8th President of the United States. German, right?"

"No, Dutch," answered Johan hesitantly.

Gillian shook their hands and smiled. "My mistake. I hope you are enjoying your stay." She turned her attention to the grandsons.

"So are you two here for the fishing tournament?"

"No, we got here too late," answered Rem, the shorter of the two. He shot a quick glance at his grandfather. Clearly not southern raised, Gillian decided. No *'yes ma'am, no sir'* in his vocabulary.

There was an awkward pause. Ralph stepped in. "But we've been out a couple of times in the Pass. We bought a 3 day license."

"Any Tarpon?" she asked.

"No," he replied.

"How about Grouper?"

Rem answered," Yes." Ralph answered, "No,"

both at the same time.

Gillian chuckled. They needed to get their stories straight.

"Well, good luck. Word to the wise: make sure you measure their length carefully if you plan on keeping any. And they shrink once on ice. Don't eyeball it. The fish and wildlife guys heavily patrol the Pass and will fine you in a heartbeat."

Rem and Ralph excused themselves and headed to the bar. Gillian returned her attention to the conversation of the remaining group. She pretended to be interested as she studied them in detail. The women took over the conversation. They all became quite chatty.

The Texans, if they were anything other than the loud, ostentatious braggers they came off as, had devised a pretty good legend. They seemed legit.

The demure, Mrs. VanBuren, slipped when she thanked the waiter by saying, *'Obrigada,'* however no one noticed. Her silk dinner suit was accessorized by a lovely brooch, encrusted with tiny white and pink stones. Gillian wondered if they were real, especially the pink ones. She thought it interesting how substituting one letter changed a surname from Dutch to German. VanBuren versus VonBuren. And wasn't Portuguese the state language of Brazil?

Then there was Nadra Patel, who abstained from the bubbly champagne, but enjoyed several of the hors d'oeuvres made with seasoned pork. A slip up hardly noticeable.

Gillian glanced at her wristwatch. "Guess I should let you get to your seats. Almost time to start. Does everyone have bidding mallets?"

Each gentleman held up what looked like a numbered table tennis paddle painted gold and black.

"Excellent. Well then, happy bidding to you all, and good luck."

On her way to the auctioneer, Gillian scrutinized the last guest as he entered the ballroom. He assessed the place like a pro; like they train you to do. He interested her. What was he up to? One thing for sure, he could certainly wear a suit.

As the auctioneer settled into the first lot, Gillian slipped through the side door and headed to the kitchen. The serving crew was outside having a smoke break, leaving Hadley alone in his castle.

"Quick. I need your help. Would you fix up a small tray of hors d'oeuvres for me? And I need a housekeeper's dress, apron and master key."

"What are you up to?" He pointed to the linen closet.

Gillian grabbed a light gray cotton dress and white apron off the shelf. "Turn around, guard the door, and I'll tell you."

Gillian slipped out of her cocktail dress and quickly buttoned the uniform. "I need to check out the invalid in Suite 203. His secretary, the creepy one with the virile face, is attending the auction. There's something dodgy about her and her boss. You know the one I'm referring to?"

"Yeah, I've seen her around. I sent Enrique up to his room yesterday morning to deliver a breakfast tray. He said the guy was covered in bandages resting in bed. He didn't respond. Guess he was still knocked out on pain killers, so he put the tray on the table and left. No tip."

"Can you keep an eye on her for me while I run up there? I mentioned to her that we'd send up a tray, but she declined, rather curtly, I might add. I shouldn't be long. If she leaves before I get back, text me."

GILLIAN GENTLY KNOCKED on the door to Suite 203 and inserted the key. "Room Service."

The room was pitch black. Gillian hesitated a moment allowing her eyes to adjust. She spotted a coffee table next to the sofa and set down the tray. Again she repeated, "Room Service," but still there was no response.

Slowly she walked to the bedroom and knocked on the door. Silence. She carefully entered and peeked inside. A body, whose face was heavily bandaged was lying on the bed. No movement though. Gillian studied the lifeless form for a moment, then walked over to the side of the bed. Without knowing, she tripped a laser encircling the bed frame, triggering a silent alarm. Gillian reached down and placed the backside of her hand an inch from the patient's nose. *Was he still breathing*, she wondered. All of a sudden the phone inside her pocket vibrated. She stepped back and glanced at the screen. The text message read, *'GET OUT NOW!'*

Gillian ran to the living room and grabbed the tray of hors d'oeuvres. She could hear the room key going in the hole on the other side. She raced to the balcony, threw the tray over the edge, and heard the door open. She froze around the corner, shielded by the outside wall. Slowly she took off her high heel shoes, slid them in her apron pocket and climbed over the left side of the balcony. Her choices were limited. It was two stories down. The neighboring balcony was ten feet away. She hoped the ornamental trellis was well anchored. She took a deep breath and leaped for the vines.

Helen Crenshaw took out a concealed knife from behind her cummerbund. She reached over to the ceramic wall plate, flipped the three switches on, and stopped.

The pungent odor of garlic greeted her. She glanced to the galley kitchen. Clean. Nothing. The room smelled like the hors d'oeuvres from the party downstairs. She grabbed her cell phone out of her pants pocket and hit a one button speed dial.

"Do you see Miss Crawford in the room?"

"No," she's not here answered Brock Hansen. "Oh, wait she just walked in. Her face looks a little flushed. Everything okay?"

"Just keep an eye on her. I think she is more than she lets on. Is the auction almost over?"

"Yes. The last painting. Lot 15 is going up now."

Gillian stood at the settlement table as the winners came forward to pay their bill, and when necessary, make shipping arrangements. Each winner was handed a small leather folder at the time of their winning bid, which they would present later to the cashier. Gillian waited impatiently for the winner of Lot 11 to appear.

"Lot 11, I believe." It was the man in the well fitted suit. "The Artist's self-portrait. Almost outbid. A lot more interest than I imagined." The late arrival guest stepped forward to the table.

Both Gillian and the female cashier, Victoria, were tongue tied. He smiled at both of them, breaking the awkward moment, and handed Gillian his folder. She looked down and smiled in furtive optimism. No doubt this wasn't the first time he had dazzled members of the opposite sex. Gillian opened his folder. A business card and check for two thousand dollars were inside. Gillian grabbed the business card and handed the folder to the cashier.

"Thank you, sir," said Victoria, sounding once again the true professional that she was. "Shall we ship the painting to the address on the check?"

"Yes, that would be best."

"Very good, sir. Thank you very much. Good night. Next?"

Before he walked away, Gillian raised her head and asked, "Excuse me, Mr. Taylor, is it? Have we met before?" His face was strangely familiar.

He shook his head. "I don't think so."

"Are you sure?" she asked quizzically, sounding as if she didn't believe him.

"I have that sort of face," he responded indifferently. "Good night, ladies. It was an interesting evening. Both the auction and the guests." He turned towards the door and walked out.

Gillian stuck the business card in her purse. She needed a moment of privacy. After the final winner had settled up, she walked down the hallway, in the direction of the lobby. She reached inside her purse and took out the card. The front side had the logo of the FBI, with a Ft. Myers address. On the back side in black ink he had written:

Please meet me at 12:30 p.m. tomorrow at this address. Come alone, and lose your tail

Max Taylor.

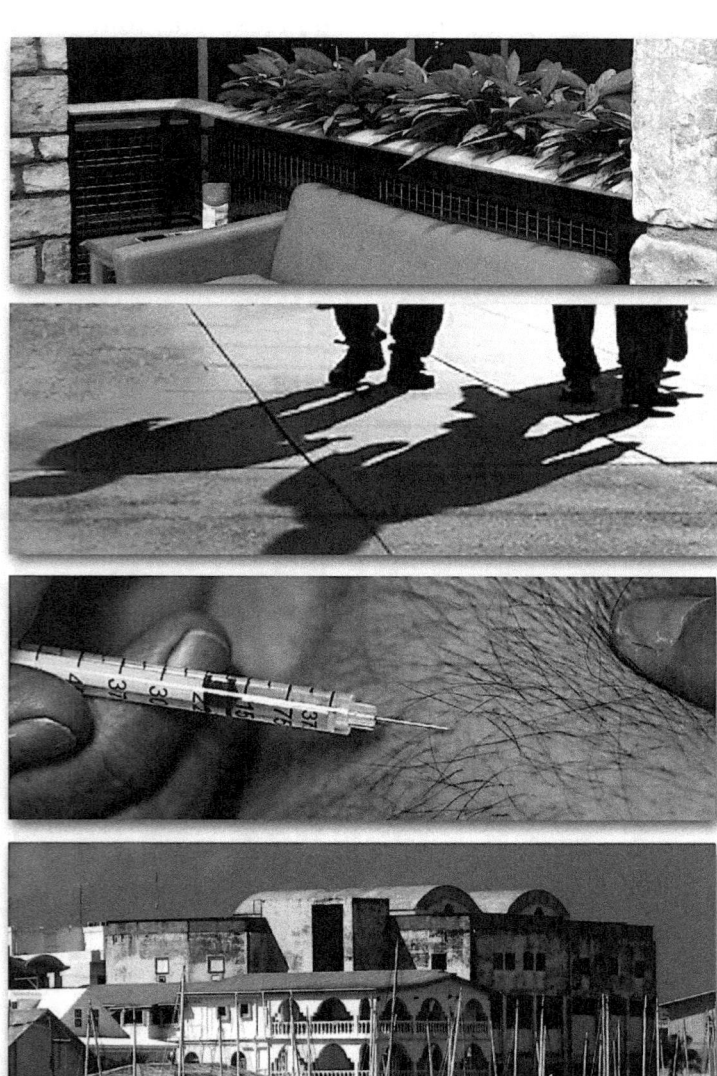

Chapter 10

Gillian arrived at the downtown office complex. It was 12:25 p.m. The reception area was a mix of leather, slate and chrome, with a light showing of ficus and palms to give it some warmth. The receptionist, a blonde, early twenties ornament, put down her emery board and checked her pink nails as Gillian approached.

"I'm here for a 12:30 appointment with Mr. Max Taylor."

"Your name, please?"

"Gillian Crawford."

The receptionist typed her name into the system, found a match, and directed her to the elevators.

"Suite 508. Last office down that hall on your left."

Gillian took the elevator to the fifth floor, all the while thinking this was not a government building. As the elevator doors opened, Max Taylor was on the other side to greet her, looking just as delicious as the night before.

"Ah, Miss Crawford. Glad you could come. Shall we?" He directed her down the hallway, then offered her a seat in his office.

"I didn't realize the FBI had offices here."

"Temporary overflow. Expansion project in the works. As you can imagine, our directive has changed significantly over the last few years.

"Yes, I suppose so." Gillian, a quick study, glanced around the room. The layout was plain. Almost stark. A desk, two chairs, computer, and a free standing coat rack. Nothing on the desk except a desk pad. No plants or family photos, only a picture of him shaking hands with the director from two administrations prior. Notwithstanding that photo op., the office was void of any personal touches, even for a man. Not even a favorite coffee cup. *This guy was clearly married to his job, and had no personal life,* she concluded.

"Well, I'll get right to the point." He slid a photograph across the desk. "Any chance you spotted this man in the last week or so?"

Gillian studied the colored glossy with interest. "No, why, should I?"

"His name is Boris Chenkov. He's a member of the Russian Mafia. Nickname: the *Mad Russian*. We believe he, or one of his operatives, killed Solomon Crawford."

"I'm sorry, what does this have to do with me?"

"We know you were friends with him."

"How so?"

"Even in this day and age, Miss Crawford, a twenty dollar bill can buy you some valuable information."

"Hmm," she replied curtly, annoyed at his condescension. This meeting wasn't going as she had hoped.

"Back to Solomon Crawford."

"You mean Vladimir Polinsky don't you," she interrupted.

His sudden delay indicated she had put him off his game.

"Right. Polinsky." He studied her face for a moment while gathering his thoughts.

"I'm going to give you a little background information, so you'll be more aware of what we're dealing with. Vladimir and Chenkov first met as teenagers during the Cold War. They went into business together when the Soviet Block dissolved, and made a butt-load of money in the black market. They ran shoulder to shoulder, tight as brothers. In fact, Vladimir's sister, Martina, was married to Chenkov's younger brother, Mikhail, who was killed by a rival crime family.

Martina and her son were devastated. She left the aegis of the family, washed her hands of them; made vindictive threats of exposing their entire business enterprise before leaving. Vladimir was put in the middle. Chenkov's ego would not tolerate a defection. He put a contract out on her but never told his partner. Years passed. There was no sign of her.

One day, a couple of years ago, she contacted her brother, Vladimir. She was terminally ill. Her liver was failing. The doctor said she had been poisoned. I'm sure you've seen similar cases in the news: Russian double agent dies. Isotope poisoning suspected. It was the same with her. Vladimir felt as if he had been kicked in the gut. His sister was dying, and his partner was responsible. Vladimir approached us, turned State's evidence, and ratted out his old friend. We were able to seize some assets, shut down some operations, but we've never been able to catch him. For what Vladimir gave us, his sister was placed at the top of the transplant list, and he entered the Witness Protection Program."

"What happened?" Gillian was absorbed at this

point.

"Sadly, she died on the operating table."

"What about her son?"

"We don't know where he is. His uncles trained him well. He's living under the radar."

Gillian was engrossed, taking it all in. Finally, she asked, "Does the dead agent, which was pulled out of the ditch a few days ago, have anything to do with this?'

"Agent Albright. Yes, he was Polinsky's original case officer."

"I thought you were."

"Excuse me?"

"I recognized your name from some newspaper in Sol's kitchen. The classified ads. I wouldn't have taken this meeting otherwise."

It was obvious he was evaluating her previous comment. "Oh-kaayyy," he paused, wondering who this lady was sitting in front of him.

"Vladimir was a low-tech kind of guy, so we used some old school means to communicate."

Gillian nodded.

He glanced down at the open folder he held in his hands.

"I understand you are old school-age friends with the local sheriff, that would be Sam Mitchell, right?"

"Yes, why?"

"Well, I imagine you'll hear about this soon enough. Agent Albright was found with ten thousand dollars on him, a deposit slip for another ninety in an offshore account, and a one way ticket to Cartagena. Planted, or maybe he went rogue. Who knows? That's why I'm here, to find out. Given his age, with that amount of cash, he could have lived like a rock star in Columbia for the rest of his life." He drummed his fingers on the desk, and thought for a moment about that lifestyle. "All we know at this time is, we have a dead federal agent, and a dead witness whom we were obligated to protect. Any help you could provide the government would certainly be appreciated."

"Like what?" she asked.

"First off, when was the last time you spoke with Vladimir?"

"Five days ago."

"How'd he seem?"

"A little preoccupied. Reticent. But sometimes he would get that way. Of course now, given what you just told me, his mood swings make a lot of sense."

"Did you two discuss anything that was bothering him?"

"No."

"Did he give you anything?"

"Like what?"

"Not sure. Maybe a key or a map."

"What exactly are you looking for, Agent Taylor?" This conversation was getting a little suspect, she thought. Gillian kept thinking about Sol's letter and the warning it contained.

"In our last contact, he mentioned some loose ends and dealing with something of value. If he gave you something, Miss Crawford, we would need to know. Your life may be in jeopardy."

Gillian shook her head and paused before looking him straight in the eye. "Sorry, I can't be of further assistance. I'm afraid there's nothing else I can think of, Agent Taylor. I do hope you find his killer and bring him to justice."

Max Taylor stood up and extended his hand. "Miss Crawford, thank you for making the trip down. If you think of anything, no matter how small, please give me a ring. Anytime. Day or night. Here's my cell number." He scratched it on the back of his business card and handed it to her.

Agent Taylor glanced at his watch. It was five minutes to one. "I'm afraid I have a departmental meeting in a few minutes, so if I may, let me walk you out."

"Please, that's not necessary. I can see myself out. Goodbye now."

Gillian made it down the elevator and out to the parking lot before realizing she had left her purse inside, under the chair. Annoyed, she turned around just in time to witness Max Taylor walk briskly out the backdoor exit. He hopped into a late model black Porsche 911 and sped away.

How the heck does a governmental employee afford a hundred and forty thousand dollar sports car, she wondered. Something was out of whack there. She remembered a lively discussion with Sol a while back about the state of the government, and what a hot mess Washington D.C. was. She used to have those same political discussions with her dad. With the two of them gone, she felt despondent, almost melancholy. Gillian recalled those endless visits to the family shrink Uncle Jack made her attend after her parents' passing. The four stages of grief: denial, depression, anger and acceptance.

Those appointments were agonizing; talking about her personal thoughts and feelings with a total stranger. She didn't want to do that again. Gillian looked up, refocused, and walked back inside the building.

After explaining, much to her embarrassment, the forgotten purse fiasco to the receptionist boy toy, Gillian went back to the elevator. This time, she and an older gentleman rode up the lift together. They both got off on the fifth floor. Gillian headed down the hallway ahead of him to the last office. She noticed the exit door Agent Taylor had just used.

Her elevator companion walked at a snail's pace behind her. As she entered the office, he spoke up and said, "May I help you, Miss?"

"Oh no. I was just here a few minutes ago for a meeting, and realized I left my purse behind. See, there it is," she pointed to the red clutch purse under the chair.

"In this office?" he asked.

"Yes, this office," Gillian responded pointedly, not understanding the confusion.

"Miss, this is my office. I'm not aware of the meeting you are referring to."

"Your office?"

"Yes, for the last two years."

"And your name would be ... ?"

"Max Taylor, of Marcella Plastics."

Gillian held her next response while she reached for her purse. The desk was now covered with files. Family photos were scattered about. The framed photograph of Agent Taylor and the Director was gone.

"I'm terribly sorry. There's been a dreadful mistake. If you'll excuse me."

Boredom is Deadly

Chapter 11

L unch on the veranda at the Boca Grande Hotel meant chilled raspberry soup, seafood salad and champagne cocktails. Gillian sat alone in the corner and enjoyed a Winston Churchill favorite: ice cold brut over a third of brandy. She finished off the cold drink and signaled the waiter for another.

She had never been good at anger management. The situation in Fort Myers with Max Taylor had left her irritated to the point of physical sentiment - punch a wall or throw something. To be played, with her eyes wide open. She didn't see it coming. Growing up, her father was steadfast in his ability to calm her down. He would frame her failure or oversight as a life lesson. She missed him desperately, especially his guidance.

Bored as usual, Gillian set out to study the afternoon lunch crowd; a few guests were gathered inside the dining hall, but most were outside on the veranda enjoying the beautiful sunny day. Low humidity, a rarity; vibrant blue, cloudless skies, and temperatures in the mid-seventies.

Today reminded her of those once-a-month Friday lunches she would have with her father, here, at this exact spot. No matter how busy he was, and no matter what was going on in his life, he always took time out for their special lunch at the hotel, followed by dessert.

The waiter would arrive with a silver platter featuring the delectable selections of the day: bananas Foster, creme brûlée, tiramisu, chocolate ganache cheesecake, and lemon cloud soufflé. But the choice was always ice cream. Ice cream was their favorite, no matter where they went.

When she was ten, her father would take her to the local convenience store where they would park out front in his pale yellow Rolls Royce convertible, eat ice cream with wooden spoons, and study the patrons as they would go in and out of the store.

"You see, Gillian, but you do not observe," Oliver Crawford would tell her. "Check out the lady that just walked by? What do you make of her?"

"Elegant dress. Must be well off," Gillian replied.

"I don't think so. Pay attention to her shoes. They are scuffed and worn. Lovely dress. Not so lovely shoes. She spent all her money on the dress, but made do with tired shoes. Now, remember the man I introduced you to as we were walking in to get ice cream? What do you make of him?"

Gillian hesitated, recalling what he looked like. "He was extremely tan. Probably spent a lot of time outside."

"Doing what?"

"Well, he had a firm grip when he shook my hand. His fingernails were broken and dirty. I'd say he was a laborer. Possibly landscaping ... and he's right handed."

"Right handed?"

"Yes. I noticed when he stood at the front entrance with his hands on his hips, his right hand was larger, more developed."

"Very good, my dear. Mr. Ramirez runs a nursery on the mainland. Double scoop of ice cream for you tomorrow."

Fond memories of her father. She cracked a smile. Gillian snapped out of her nostalgic fog when Hadley arrived and pulled up a chair. She was now in the middle of her meal.

"Based on the numbers I received from Father Flannigan this morning, I'd say the auction was a big success."

"Thanks for your help," she responded. "Interesting buyers last night. Several were sizing up more than just artwork. By the way, your appetizers were magnifique, even though some landed on the back lawn."

Hadley gave her a questioning frown but did not ask. "I was a little concerned we would run out of the foie gras, but we managed. No leftovers for you, though."

Hadley slowly combed the veranda. "Keep talking and smile," he whispered in a directing tone. "I have something for you."

He placed his hands in the middle of the table. Gillian spotted a small composite object concealed in the palm of his hand. Her hands moved on top of his as they managed the exchange. An air kiss was added as she played up their affection.

"From this morning's breakfast crowd. Thought you might be interested."

Gillian put the wireless earpiece in and nodded. Hadley reached into his black pants pocket and turned on the MP3 Player. The first voice she heard was masculine.

"We can't find his boat, the Tokyo Rose, or get into his house. It's still an active crime scene. We do know he was seriously low-tech: no credit cards, mobile phone, internet. No friends, except for a local by the name of Gillian Crawford. We tapped her house. Our eyes and ears lasted a whopping twenty-four hours before a crew arrived, swept the place and pulled the plug." The conversation stopped without a reply. A one sided chat. *Maybe he was on a cell phone,* Gillian reasoned.

On the next track were two new voices. The first one was low, with a Russian accent. Gillian looked up at Hadley and frowned. Her hands began to fidget.

"You need to apply pressure on her. Make her hurt."

"We already have. I warned her."

"Well, go back and apply more," he snapped. "Find out what she knows. Maybe she's found his damn boat."

Gillian started to speak, but Hadley interrupted. "Hang on. There's a few more."

"Some interested parties have arrived." The slower cadence of his words made him sound old. "The Geiger counter will be here shortly. Our boy wonder managed to hack into the local co-op. He'll take down the Grid at twenty-two hundred hours. You'll have fourteen minutes max before the system resets. Bing, bang, out. Remember no evidence we set foot on the property. Are we clear?"

Hadley held up three more fingers. Gillian glanced out onto the croquet lawn as Hadley cued up the next track. A threesome was playing the final round of the course: Miss Crenshaw, with Christine and Brock Hansen. An odd mix. They seemed to be engaged in a heated discussion with hands flying in sync with their tongues.

The next sound byte started up. This one was a male who sounded a little raspy. "That hit on the FBI Agent has made things more difficult. Curiosity and investigative levels are way up. Especially that busy-body ... Francesca, what's her name again?"

"Gillian Crawford," said a voice with a European accent.

"I think you should take the plane back up. Perhaps he beached her in a remote cove."

There was another break followed by two new voices: a man and a woman.

"Where did they take the body?" asked the man in an irritated tone.

"Vladimir's or Albright's?"

"Vladimir's. Find out which law firm is handling his Estate. Who the executor and heirs are. Dig deeper. I shouldn't have to hold your hand."

Hadley waited for Gillian to look up.

"Okay, here's the last one," he said.

"As soon as I can take care of this, we'll be out of here. It's not easy to find someone who can handle the volume we're talking about. It's too risky. I need to make sure everything is lined up, so when the time comes, we can move quickly."

Gillian downed her second glass of champagne before she spoke. "Do you have faces to go with these sound bytes? I don't recognize any of their voices. My suspect list must be way off."

"The morning chatter doesn't help the recording quality, plus, when people whisper, they sometimes sound different."

Gillian nodded.

"As for faces, we have a problem," Hadley confessed sheepishly. "The busboy got a little over zealous this morning since we were so busy. He cleared the tables before I could match them up. Room charges and video feeds are all I can offer. Both inconclusive and time consuming."

"Did the sound bytes come from different tables?"

"Yes, but the tables flip on average three times each morning. So the guests could have come and gone and come back again. Sorry."

Gillian frowned as she tried to connect the dots. "Still ... it helps. We know more than before. First off, the person who mugged me is going to try again." Gillian held up another finger with each new point. "There's a female by the name of Francesca. The Kamikaze pilot is going back up to search for Sol's boat. I wonder how they know he had a boat, and why are they so curious about it, unless they are the ones who stole my letter, ergo, they're the ones that broke into my house and bugged the place. Lastly, there's someone who is doing what I would do: examine Sol's assets and follow the money trail."

"I wonder how the system works, when the government puts you into Witness Protection," Hadley asked. "I bet if you examine the property records it would show shell corporation, after shell corporation. Do you suppose he actually had any assets?"

"Besides a cache of diamonds, and enough fission material to create a wasteland," she replied.

"True. Interesting balance sheet," Hadley responded back while trying not to smile. She glanced at him cross-eyed and shook her head.

"What do you think about the sound byte that referred to acquiring something valuable that they'd need to unload in a hurry?"

"They need a fence," he answered.

"I need to get into Sol's house and have another look around before the island-wide blackout at ten o'clock tonight, compliments of a hacker, who's associate can get his hands on a Geiger counter in a hurry. Not exactly an item you can pick up at your local hardware store."

Gillian stood up and threw her napkin on the table.

"Where are you going?" he asked.

"I need a refresher course in rudimentary physics."

"That can't be good."

"I'll see you before the lights go out."

AN HOUR LATER, at the far side of the visitor's parking lot, was a black Cadillac Escalade with limo tint windows. The engine was running. The air conditioner was pumping full blast.

The jewelry clad ogre was sitting behind the driver's seat using his cell phone. "She's changed vehicles. Now she's driving a dark blue Maserati. Sweet ride."

"Where are you," a younger voice asked from the other end.

Silence.

"Yuri, you there? Yuri? Hello."

"I'm in the parking lot of a school."

"Name?"

"It's ... Eisenhower. Eisenhower High School.

Figures. Imperialist Americans. Always honoring their warlords. What are you doing?"

More silence.

"Nikolay, can you hear me? Freakin' signal." He glanced at his phone's LCD screen and signal bars.

"Give me a second. I'm running a cross check between the Crawford lady and teachers on staff."

Nikolay's dark, lifeless eyes were the occupational result from endless hours he spent in front of a computer. Yuri's creepy sidekick had set up a command post in a junior suite, on the top floor of the Boca Grande Hotel: four laptops, side by side, curtains drawn, power cords running everywhere. A split screen displayed Gillian Crawford's dossier he had compiled on the left, albeit some unfortunate gaps. On the right, scrolled a list of the administrative staff.

"Got it. Anthony Mitchell," Nikolay pointed to the bottom of the screen. "Both studied at Oxford. They had an overlapping year. He left first. Got a job at a commercial laboratory in Virginia. Wrote some well received papers on isotope transfer. Was granted a patent for a molecular structure analysis machine they use in crime labs that set him up financially for life. Appears he decided to leave the corporate jungle and give back to the community. So now he teaches."

"What subject?" asked Yuri.

"Honors physics. He's the department chair."

"Looks like the Fed's didn't get both birdcages after all. Just as Boris suspected," he shook his head. "Vladimir's insurance policy - in case the American's didn't play fair. Contact Boris and let him know.

Find out if he wants me to pick up the Crawford bitch."

Nikolay hung up, chugged his third energy drink of the day, then walked down the hall to the elevator.

Chapter 12

The Foggy Bottom Bar was a hole-in-the-wall establishment not far from the marina; a watering hole for the locals at quitting time. Its decor included quintessential driftwood, business cards tacked to the wall, recessed rope lighting along the floor, and amber candle globes on each table. They served cold beer, bottom shelf hard liquor and black coffee, pretty much in that order. On Saturdays, a forgettable three piece local band provided the musical entertainment. During the week, songs were piped in through the bartender's MP3 player.

Gillian, running late, rushed into the bar a few minutes past 6 p.m. She paused as her eyes adjusted to the darkness. She had arranged to have cocktails with an old friend of her father's, Crandle Eastman, a local architect with accolades out the wazoo. Now in his golden years, he worked only when something interesting crossed his desk. Projects for Jonathan Cromwell he found interesting. Lately though, most of his time was spent having cocktails with lonely, rich widows who had too much time on their hands.

"Good to see you, Gillian." He pecked her politely on the side of her cheek. "How's my favorite secret agent these days?"

Gillian frowned, as she glanced around to see who was in earshot. "I have no idea what you're referring to, Crandle. But I'm well. Thanks for asking."

He ordered her a dirty martini with two olives. "Sorry to hear about Solomon Crawford. Such an interesting chap. Did a little work for him when he first moved here. I remember seeing a photograph of the two of you in the newspaper a while back, winners of a fishing tournament."

"Yes. Last Fall. We caught a dozen bull dolphin in one afternoon. My wrists ached for days afterwards, but the outing was worth it. We had a tremendous time."

"I suppose the sheriff has his hands full at the moment. A bunch of damn Yankees giving him their two cents about how he should handle the investigation. I suspect they don't think law enforcement in a podunk town amounts to much."

"I'm sure he'll set them straight," she said.

"Oh, before I forget, here are those plans I drew up for your uncle's island. I take it you'll critique them, using your ... tradecraft, and get back with me on any relevant changes. This should be interesting." Crandle raised his eyebrows following his pompous inference.

Gillian smiled thinly and put the rolled up blueprints down beside her feet. She downed the martini and signaled the waitress for another. His earlier comment had just sunk in.

"Rough day?" he asked.

She ignored his question. "What kind of work did you do for Sol?"

"I don't remember," he replied, and waved his hand as if to dismiss her unimportant question. "Small renovation, I think."

"Funny, I don't remember any construction."

"Prior to you meeting him, I believe." Crandle was becoming disinterested.

"Do you think you could search back in your records?"

He set down his glass of Scotch and stared her straight in the eye. "Probably not." His reply was blunt, full of innuendo.

Gillian tried to get a read on what he would not say.

Finally, Crandle smiled and stood up. "Oh, look who's arrived. My dinner date."

Lizzie Hancock, the local psychic, was in her mid-sixties, had flaming red hair, wore turquoise blue eye shadow and shiny, coral lipstick. Thirty years ago, she was a full-time resident at the Boca Grande Hotel. Cromwell had seen to it. Rumor was, he was returning a favor. She worked evenings mostly. Her psychic readings were more popular during the late-night hours. Afterwards, emotionally exhausted, she would get sauced up on whiskey, feel lonely, and dial zero to chat with the local telephone operators who worked the graveyard shift. One of her clients, a wealthy one, left her a sizable sum upon his death, allowing her to move to her own little cottage not far from the lighthouse. Business was mainly by telephone these days, little foot traffic, but she was fine with the change.

"Lizzie Hancock, you know Gillian Crawford, I believe."

"Yes, it's been a while." Lizzie greeted her with a lower class, upper class guarded smile; unsure as to what to say next.

Gillian shook her hand and gave Crandle a curious nod. Clearly their relationship was not of an intellectual nature.

Crandle, being a complete gentleman, plugged the awkward silence. "You look lovely, my dear." He reached out and kissed her hand. "We were conversing about what happened to Solomon Crawford."

"Hmm, yes," Lizzie began. "A lot of bad karma in the air that night. I didn't sleep well. The business phone was unusually quiet. I went to bed early but couldn't sleep; a neighbor's dog was barking. I remember going out on the back deck after midnight to get some fresh air. That's when I spotted a man running down the beach. Frightening sight that time of night."

"You should have called me, Lizzie. I would have come over."

Gillian feigned a cough and glanced at Crandle.

"Were you acquainted with Solomon?" he asked.

"Yes, professionally as a matter-of-fact. Quite recently. About two weeks ago we had a few private readings. He was interested in a nephew he'd lost touch with, and a sister who had passed over. The first session was particularly sad because I couldn't help him. I was blocked. I can't fill you in on all the details. A lot of what my clients tell me is sacred, like priests and confessions. As soon as he opened up though, and concentrated on some sequestered feelings, I was able to channel his sister, and advise him on a future meeting with his nephew. He seemed more at peace after our last session, which is always a good thing."

Before the conversation headed into the psychic realm of medium divination, Gillian grabbed the drawings and stood to leave.

"Well, I must be going. Thank you for the blueprints. I'll get back with you in a day or two. Nice seeing you again, Miss Lizzie. Enjoy your evening."

Gillian got into her car and drove over to Sol's house. She wanted to take a look inside. If her hunch was right, Crandle had designed a panic room for Sol and had cleverly camouflaged the addition. She bet a confidentiality agreement was likely involved. When she turned the final corner onto his street, her headlights landed on a patrol car in the driveway.

"Figures," she said out loud. Sam was all over this. She made a three-point turn and headed for the police station.

The sheriff hung up the phone when she entered his office. Gillian could play him whenever she wanted. He was too easy. The worried expression on her face was all that was needed.

"You all right?" he asked, sounding concerned.

"Yes, but I've had a break in at the house."

"When?"

"Last night."

"Before or after you came over."

"Before."

He knew something was up. "You're getting around to telling me a day later?"

"I knew you were tied up with this murder investigation, so ... ."

"Those scratches on your face." He pointed to her forehead. It was more a statement than a question.

"No, honestly, they have nothing to do with the break-in. I'm not even lying."

Only from her would that be amusing, he thought. "Did they take anything? What about your alarm system? Wasn't it armed?" He was firing off questions quicker than she could respond.

"Some money, maybe a thousand bucks, and one of my cameras. I've had the locks changed. Been with the insurance company most of the day trying to inventory valuables. They advised me to file a report with you. I believe a few first edition books are missing, although I'm not entirely sure. Seems to me I loaned them to Sol a while back, but can't remember if he returned them. I was wondering if we could drive over to his house so I might check."

"Gillian, his place is a crime scene. Can't this wait?"

"I know this is a lot to ask, but they were my father's. It would mean a lot to me. I promise I won't touch anything. You'll be right next to me, supervising my every move." The pleading look on her face was too much. He caved.

"All right. I'll take you over, but you can't remove anything. If you see them, you let me know. I'll make sure they get back to you once we're done. Agreed?"

"Yes. You're a sweetheart. Thank you, Sam." Gillian smiled warmly and hugged him a little longer than usual.

Sam cleared his throat and straightened his tie. "Come on then, let's go and get this over with."

They arrived by patrol car at Sol's house a few minutes later. The property was blocked off by yellow police tape. The young patrolman on duty sat up straight when he spotted them in his rear view mirror.

"Evening, Sheriff. Ma'am."

"Doyle, all quiet?"

"Yes, sir."

"Good, let's keep it that way. We'll be right back."

"Yes, sir."

"Do I know him?" she whispered as they proceeded up the sidewalk.

"New academy graduate, on loan from Ft. Myers."

"Wow, he's young. I wonder if this is his first assignment."

"Probably."

Gillian followed the sheriff up the steps to the living quarters on the second floor. He turned on his flashlight and entered the living room. Gillian walked carefully around and stopped in front of the bookcase. The shelves were full. Sol was an avid reader. A history buff, as she recalled. She pointed to three on the middle shelf: Christie, Dickens and Faulkner.

"What a relief," she sighed. "I would hate to have something happen to them." She turned around and took a calculating glance around the room. As she moved towards the back deck, the sheriff reached out and blocked her progress with his arm.

"Can't go past this point, Gillian. Sorry."

"Oh, right. What was I thinking? Well then. That's really all I needed. Thank you again. I'll sleep better now."

When Gillian and the sheriff walked across the stone driveway, she pretended to lose her footing and started to fall. Sam grabbed her quickly and held her in his arms.

"You okay?" he asked in earnest.

"My ankle. Rolled the bloody thing." A few British colloquiums from her Oxford days stayed with her.

"Here, lean on me."

Gillian held onto his arm as they walked towards the patrolman. She sold the act. The young rookie could tell they were clearly into one another.

"Okay, Doyle. It's all yours. Keep a sharp eye out tonight. I don't think we'll get any visitors, but you never can be too vigilant."

"Yes, sir. Will do."

Gillian smiled at the young rookie and said good night. He tipped his hat to her in reply.

Sam dropped Gillian off at the hotel and reminded her to ice her ankle. "Your car will be safe at the police station until morning," he said.

She balked at first, then agreed; otherwise her insistence would have appeared too suspicious. Gillian pretended to favor her left foot as she walked gingerly towards the entrance. At the top of the steps, she turned and waved good-bye, then entered the hotel lobby. She watched him pull away then made a dash for Hadley's kitchen.

Hadley stood up from a wooden stool and smiled. "I was expecting a visit from you earlier this evening. You okay? Can I get you something to eat?"

"Not now, but you can make me a little to-go box. Something manly. Meat and potatoes, and sprinkle some of that CH stuff over the top."

"You mean, Chloral Hydrate?"

"Yeah, that."

"Pretty strong stuff. What makes you think I have some?"

"You say kitchen, I say chem-lab. It's all the same." They both cracked a smile.

"I've gotta run over to Sol's for a few minutes. Oh, and I need to borrow your Beemer."

"How do you think you're going to gain access. You know his place is a crime scene. I heard a patrol car is parked in his driveway."

"A bribe naturally. That's what the food is for. Trust me. I'll be back in thirty minutes."

He held up his car keys, with a doubtful look on his face.

"Don't worry about your precious ride. I'll be careful."

"You know I trust you. It's just when you get behind a steering wheel the little gray cells in your head malfunction."

"Oh, please. I'm not that pathetic."

"Come on. I'll drive. You can fill me in on the rest of your plan. If anything, I can distract the patrolman and buy you some more time. Who's on duty, Gus?"

"No, his name is Doyle. New kid. Very young. Straight out of the academy."

Moments later they pulled in behind the patrol car in Hadley's 633i. Gillian, faking a sprained left ankle, walked gimpy towards the driver's side of the patrol car. Hadley was a few steps behind.

"Bet you're surprised to see me," she began. "I feel like such a dummy, but I left my purse inside. Would you mind terribly if I go back up and get it? I promise to only be a minute."

Before he was able to answer, Gillian added, "Oh yes, Hadley and I brought you this." She thrust the little to-go box in his face. "We thought you might be hungry. Hadley's the head chef over at the Boca Grande Hotel. Smells delicious, don't you think?" She opened the box and swirled the container around to bring out the aroma.

Hadley butted in. "It's a New York strip with béarnaise sauce, and a side of Garlic Mashed Potatoes. Nothing worse than being hungry, on duty, and unable to leave."

He was starving. "Well, I suppose the sheriff won't mind." He reached for the door handle and got out. "Just remember, like he said, don't touch anything." You need help up the stairs?"

"No, I'm good. I'll just be a moment. Hadley, you keep him company, eh?"

"Sure, no problem."

"So, how do you think the Rays are going to fare this year? You get to watch any spring training?"

The young officer, distracted by the question, paused at the end of the car. Hadley had strategically moved ever so slowly and blocked his path to the house. Doyle considered following, but let her go. Hadley's attempt at engaging conversation had worked.

Gillian made her way up the steps, surprised that Hadley followed baseball. He was good at improvising. That's what made him incredibly valuable in the field: journalist in Beirut, history professor in Algiers, he particularly liked the co-eds, archeologist in the Kashmir Valley. Adapt. He would always do that.

As she entered the living room, Gillian eyed the wall partition between the living room, hallway, and adjoining bedroom. The space was off about six and a half feet on the bedroom side. When she walked by the sealed fireplace, the painting above the mantel caught her eye: a sailboat, pitched slightly in calm seas, fitted with full sails. A common nautical setting. Nothing special. In fact, she had never paid the artwork much attention, but something in her gut made her curious. Gillian leaned closer and read the name on the boat's mainsail. In faded black letters - 'Tokyo Rose.' She had a flashback of that dilapidated picture frame at Sol's yacht basin slip. Her pulse quickened. Gillian lifted the bottom of the frame away from the wall and spotted a secret button. Just as she was about to push it, she heard a pair of footsteps coming up the stairs.

"Miss Crawford, is everything all right?"

She grabbed her purse and grinned. "Got it. I'm coming." It was on to Plan B.

Chapter 13

Hadley parked his car in front of a vacant lot around the corner from Sol's house. A dark spot between two street lights.

"Is this far enough?" he asked.

"Perfect."

"Did you find anything?"

"Looks like Crandle retrofitted a safe room for Sol. I believe it's behind his old fireplace."

"What?" he asked in disbelief. "You're kidding me."

Gillian's expression was grave.

"A secret passageway?" Hadley chuckled. "What is this, Masterpiece Theater?"

"I'm just telling you what I found," she stated matter-of-factly. "How long will it take for that drug to kick in?"

"Metabolized with meat and potatoes, I'd say fifteen minutes." He glanced at his wristwatch: 9:39 p.m. They were running out of time.

Hadley grabbed a pair of night vision goggles from the trunk of his car. A handy little gadget he had permanently absconded from his previous employer. The two of them made their way through the scrub brush until they arrived at the tree line which abutted Sol's yard. Gillian swatted mosquitoes while Hadley adjusted the lenses. He spotted Officer Doyle loosening his tie and tilting his seat back. It wouldn't be long now.

"You sure you want to do this? It's less than twenty minutes till the black out."

"I'll use the stairs on the back side of the house. No one will notice. Stop worrying so much."

Hadley reached out, lifted her chin and looked her square in the eyes. "I feel compelled to remind you we are both private citizens now, lest you forget."

Gillian rolled her eyes. "If they arrive before I get out, make some noise."

Hadley scoured the perimeter one last time. The young police officer was out. Eyes shut, head back, mouth wide open. Hadley gave her the all clear.

Gillian made her way around the back of the house, avoiding the front entrance. On the ground floor, was a wooden door to the concealed stairwell that led upstairs. The entry was locked. She pulled a small leather pouch from her pants pocket and retrieved two small instruments: a tension wrench and a hook pick.

Picking locks was an old hobby of hers. She had become interested in the internal mechanisms at a very young age and later on, had excelled in the finer techniques, thanks to Hadley, her mentor. They use to race one another cracking safes, but their rivalry stopped after she beat him a time or two. Boredom was boring. She thought about Uncle Jack's comment the other morning, during their very early chat. This clandestine stuff was in her blood. He was right.

Gillian held the tip of the little black flashlight in her mouth and shined the beam on the lock. She placed the tension wrench in the lower portion of the keyhole and applied some torque. In went the hook pick, and with a couple nudges to the pins, voila, the lock was opened. She glanced over her shoulder and quietly slipped inside.

The top of the steps came out onto the back deck, six feet from where the blood pool had stained the flooring. The sight unnerved her. Gillian froze. She had witnessed some horrific things in her prior life, none of which were personal. Back then it was all professionally categorized, with no emotional attachment. A buffer. The crime scene at her feet was personal. She could hear Hadley's voice inside her head warning her of personal involvement; of retribution. It would not end well, he once told her. Sage wisdom bestowed by him when they first worked together. Back when he felt compelled to nurture her conscience as she delved into the business.

Gillian turned the corner towards the living room and headed for the fireplace. She reached up, lifted the painting from the wall and pushed the access button. There was a gush of air around her feet as the back wall of the fireplace rotated ninety degrees, revealing the entrance.

She had to duck to enter the safe room. The space was about ten by six located between the living room and bedroom. Probably once a walk in closet. The walls were concrete, an eight inch thick access door was enclosed in steel, with a brick veneer facade. Gillian shined her flashlight around the room. One chair, a small refrigerator, and a surveillance system, with a butt load of monitors: front door, the driveway, living room, rear deck. No unwelcome guests in sight. She could make out Officer Doyle sleeping in his patrol car. Gillian took two steps back and collided with a compact table in the corner. Lying on top was a black velvet satchel with a pull string closure, and a bright chrome canister the size of a small camping lantern. The lettering around the outside was Cyrillic.

The magnitude of her find made her hands tremble. She grabbed the velvet pouch and stuffed it in her pocket. As she reached out to touch the birdcage, a man's hand came around her face and smothered her mouth.

Gillian's scream was muffled as she tried to bolt.

"They're here," he whispered in her ear. It was Max Taylor. "Three men with weapons, coming in hot."

She recognized his voice and froze.

"Kill the light and shut us in. You better pray this room lives up to its name." He released her.

Gillian's reaction was instantaneous. She punched the door switch then turned to face him.

"What the bloody hell are you doing here?" she whispered in a contemptuous fit. She was pissed and could not control her temper. "And don't tell me you're with the FBI, or that your name is Max Taylor, because I know they're damn lies."

Before he could respond the electricity went off, and the monitors shut down. The room went pitch black. So black Gillian could not see an inch in front of her nose. Max touched a side button on his wristwatch to illuminate its face. Ten o'clock, straight up. The backup system kicked in, with the surveillance cameras online a minute later. The two of them viewed the monitors as three men with AR-15 Assault Rifles rushed up the driveway, past the sleeping patrolman.

"I saw them drive by, circle back, and park along the beach road. Your friend, hiding in the woods, must have spotted them too and doubled back to his car. So much for your calvary. And you're right, I'm not Agent Max Taylor. My name is Illarion Chenkov. Illarion is Russian for the Greek name, Hilarion. So I go by Harry. The surname, Stevens, is a lot easier. American as apple pie. No red flags. I knew your friend long before he took the name Crawford. He was my uncle. My mother's brother. He was in trouble and needed my help. But I was too late. Now I owe it to him to find out what happened."

She pointed to the canister, and asked in a stoic whisper, "Did you come for this?"

"Is that what I think it is?"

She nodded her head. A drop of sweat rolled down the side of her face.

"Whatever's going to happen will be over in the next few minutes. When that young police officer misses his hourly check-in, your buddy, the sheriff, will dispatch all available emergency personnel to this location. Just curious, how many will be coming to our rescue? One or two? What did you drug the young officer with, by the way?"

Gillian tilted her head, feigning a confused expression on her face, but did not reply.

He pointed to the upper right monitor. "Recognize any of those men?"

"The lead guy carrying the yellow box, yes. I wonder what that is?" Gillian knew perfectly well but played clueless. She went to school with the inventor's great-grandson.

"That would be a Geiger counter," he replied

stoically.

"Yes, I recognize him, Ralph VanBuren. He and his brother, Rem, are guests at the hotel. They are here with their grandparents, Tilla and Johan VanBuren."

"New playmates of yours?"

Ralph and Rem VanBuren, along with another man Gillian didn't recognize, rush into the living room then immediately disperse. Ralph made his way slowly around the corner with the box and went off screen. His brother went to the rear of the house while the other guy stayed posted at the front door.

"Unless there's been a leak, between the protection of the birdcage and the containment of these concrete walls, he won't get any readings. On the other hand, if there is, the party's over for all of us. Poison is a Russian payback, you know. Maybe its what my uncle had in mind all along."

Gillian cast a grim look his way.

"If these men did business with my uncle, they're ruthless. They won't give up until they get what they came for. I can assure you."

Gillian's eyes stayed glued to the monitors as they continued to search the house. Cushions, pillows, books, lamps. Anything touched was put back in its place. Gillian pointed to the living room monitor as one of the men pulled picture frames off the wall looking for hidden safes. It was only a matter of time before they would make the discovery.

Meanwhile, Hadley, seeing all three intruders enter the house, made his way over to their car. A late edition black, Mercedes SUV. The vehicle was unlocked with the windows lowered. He opened the door, sat down, and ripped the cover off the inside electrical system below the steering wheel.

Rem VanBuren walked back to the living room. They were running out of time. He glanced at the painting over the fireplace. It was the last one to check. The young man walked over to the mantel and reached for the frame.

Inside the panic room, Gillian was losing her nerve. By merely shutting the access door, had she secured the room, as well? Harry and Gillian stared at the monitor as the younger VanBuren spotted the button and gave it a push. Her heart stopped.

Outside, Hadley was still in the SUV mumbling to himself. "Make some noise, you say? I'll make some noise. How do you like this?" He yanked several wires from below the instrument panel, separated the red from the green and yellow, and severed them with his knife.

The car's security system sounded off, piercing the quiet, late hour with an alarming racket. "Wake up, Doyle," he said out loud. "Go do your duty."

Gillian and Harry Stevens watched as all three men immediately stopped. Rem pointed to the access button. Ralph aimed his gun at the spot and fired off several shots. The button shred to pieces, but nothing else happened. By now, the car alarm was competing with a police siren. Ralph VanBuren signaled them to leave thru the rear of the house.

"Look, something's spooked them," she said. "Can you hear that? It sounds like a car alarm."

The camera on the rear deck caught two of the men running down the back stairs. Ralph VanBuren reached inside his jacket pocket and pulled out three small canisters and threw them on the floor.

The dynamics changed quickly. Smoke and tear gas swept through each room. The cottage was engulfed with a toxic agent. Gillian spotted Hadley on a monitor signaling her to fly away, followed by Officer Doyle, now jolted out of his drug laden sleep, calling for backup.

"There's my cue, Harry Stevens, or Max Taylor, or whatever your name is. I'll be seeing you." Gillian reached over and grabbed the birdcage. He placed his hand on top of hers.

"We both know how this is going to play out," he began. "Neither one of us is going to walk out of here alone. I don't trust you, and you sure as hell don't trust me. We're going out together, so stay close, and try to keep up."

Chapter 14

Gillian tucked the canister under her left arm, and never looked back. Who was keeping up with whom, she mused. She was a local who knew the island's layout like the back of her hand. Gillian zig-zagged her way out of Sol's neighborhood unnoticed, without incident and with remarkable speed.

Six blocks from his house, Gillian stopped to catch her breath. She had made it to the parking lot of the public beach. The location was pitch black. The street lights had yet to reset. She bent over and put her hands on her knees. Her lungs burned, her head was dizzy.

"Why are you stopping?" Her uninvited shadow appeared by her side.

She stood up and scoured the parking lot. The place was empty. "Feel free ... to ... go," she replied with a directional gesture.

He glanced down at the pavement where the canister was wedged between her feet.

Gillian shook her head.

"This way," he said. "As it happens, my car's right over there."

Gillian peered at him incredulously, but followed him to the black Porsche she had spotted him in yesterday.

"Freakin' smoke!" Tears were pouring down her face. "How is it you're not affected? My eyes feel like ... ."

"Shards of glass in them," he interrupted.

"Something like that."

"Smoke bomb laced with tear gas. Here, this will help."

Harry reached into his car and grabbed an unopened bottle of water. "Lean your head back." He grabbed the back of her head and poured the water over her eyes. She struggled to break free, but he held her firm. "Keep them open," he yelled.

She coughed up water, then spit on the ground.

"Better?" he asked as he tossed her a turquoise beach towel.

She nodded.

"Don't rub them. We need to get out of these clothes. They're contaminated." He started to remove his shirt.

Her slanted brow spoke volumes.

He stopped. "All right, the hotel it is."

"You're staying there?" she asked.

He nodded. "But what about ... ?" Harry pointed to the canister

"They have a safe at the hotel."

"I don't think so. I've done my homework. A little waitress told me about your family connection."

Harry remained silent as they raced down the dark, damp road towards the center of town. The cool, sea breeze blowing across on his face, helped clear his head.

An idea hit him. He slammed on the breaks. His right arm flew out to save her from the dashboard as the car fishtailed to a halt.

"Are you out of your mind," she yelled.

He calmly replied, "Are you a woman of faith, Miss Crawford?"

"Why?" She snapped back. The smell of burnt rubber permeated the air.

"Do you know the local priest?"

His line of questioning was irritating. "Yes, I'm a woman of faith. Yes, I know the local priest. His name is Father Flannigan."

"Well enough to call in a favor?"

Gillian replied curiously, "I suppose so."

"All right then." Harry made a three point turn and drove slowly into the parking lot of the Catholic Church, St. Michael's. He turned off the engine. The parking lot was empty. A peaceful, quiet setting disturbed only by the evening ensemble of tree frogs and the occasional loon. The two of them got out of the car, with the canister now wrapped in a towel. Harry followed Gillian as they walked to the vicarage and rang the doorbell.

Father Flannigan cracked opened the door holding a lit candle in his hand. He was dressed in gray sweatpants and a Notre Dame t-shirt.

"Gillian," he began, clearly confused. "What on earth? Is everything all right?" He squinted his eyes as he ran his fingers through his hair, directing it in place.

"Father, I'm so sorry to call this late. I need to ask a favor of you. I'm afraid it's rather important. May we come in?"

"Yes, yes, of course. By all means." He unhooked the door chain and stood aside. The inside lights flickered. Gillian wondered if she had just witnessed a sign.

"Can you hold onto something for a day or two? Oh, let me introduce you first to Harry Stevens. He is

... was ... Solomon Crawford's nephew."

"An honor to meet you, Father." Harry extended his hand.

"Please have a seat. It appears our blackout is over." He blew out the candle. "May I offer you some refreshments?"

"No, thank you, Father."

Gillian moseyed around the room as Father Flannigan offered his condolences. She stopped in front of an old, upright piano that she had never heard played. Her fingers touched the ivories then paused. Gillian realized at that moment, this would be her last visit. She would need to disappear too, just like Sol had planned. No more tea with cake on rainy afternoons with Father Francis. It had always fascinated her how grounded and unwavering he was. He, on the other hand, told her many times how much he enjoyed her curiosity. She raised the lid of the upright and slid the canister deep inside, along the soundboard.

Gillian turned towards the two men as Harry asked the other point blank. "We can count on you, to keep the package?"

"And keep this between ourselves," she said. "Let me add, I wouldn't touch it either. Not a good thing." She shook her head.

Father Flannigan looked expressionless at both of them and sighed.

Gillian added, "We'll be back to claim our stash in a day or two." She had positioned herself between Harry and Father Francis, winked and mouthed the words, *"I will."*

The priest scratched his head and nodded in

agreement.

"All right then, we best be off. Thank you, Father," Harry said as he stood to leave.

"I trust you two are not in any trouble."

They glanced at one another, but said nothing.

Father Flannigan knew Gillian well enough to discern she was in a difficult state of affairs, with a stranger no less, who showed up out of nowhere. And what was with that horrible smell? He put his hands on her shoulders, peered down at her face and whispered softly. "God be with you, my dear," and kissed the top of her head.

"Let's hope so, Father. Good Night."

A few minutes later, back at the hotel, Gillian and Harry entered through the service entrance and went up the staff stairwell.

They smelled like rotten eggs; lingering trace from the tear gas. Gillian was eager to strip off her clothes and soak in a tub. They agreed to meet downstairs in the lounge in about an hour to hash things out.

He was an odd bean, she thought. Attractive. Street smart. Guarded. Obvious trust issues. She had her agenda. She needed to see how her plans stacked up with his. Sometimes the complexities of the strategic process were seriously misunderstood. Simple was usually the best course of action. If she couldn't outsmart him, there was always the power of the little black dress. She had seen female sexuality work more times than she'd care to admit.

When Gillian arrived at the first floor lounge, wearing a form fitting black cocktail dress, and Louboutin stiletto heels, a waiter led her to a private covered balcony that overlooked the reflection pool at the south end of the hotel.

Someone had been busy. White, privacy drapes blew gently in the breeze. Set out were a dozen or so lit candles, a magnum of champagne chilling and Beluga caviar for two. A soundtrack of Miles Davis provided the finishing touch.

Harry Stevens turned from the railing when she arrived. He had changed into a dark suit, white shirt, no tie. He smiled and offered her a seat. The connection between them was electric. Gillian sensed his warm breath on the back of her neck as he helped her with her chair. Her nerves jumped.

"Feeling better?" he asked. His finger ran down the side of her arm.

"Much," she replied, saying nothing further. Her inner voice was saying, *'Bet I could make you feel better too.'* She held back a smile.

"I believe we got off to a bad start," he began. "I was hoping we might try again."

"Me too." She ran the tip of her tongue over her bottom lip.

He popped the cork of the champagne bottle and poured them each a glass of Dom.

The label was not unnoticed by her.

"How long has it been since you've seen your uncles?" she began.

"I was twelve when my mother and I left Moscow. I haven't seen or heard from Boris since. As for Vladimir, he contacted me about a week ago."

"Do you think you'd recognize him? Boris, I mean."

"It's been seventeen years. When I was young, I

would spend nearly every afternoon of my life with him, learning the family business. I was closer to Vladimir though. He took me camping and fishing. Bought me my first gun. They both had a penchant for business. Vladimir liked the outdoors. Boris loved the theater. The opera in particular. I doubt he would recognize me though. Too much time has passed, and I was just a kid. I've lived under the radar for so long. I'd like to keep it that way." He downed the glass of champagne and poured himself another.

He continued. "Look, my plans are quite simple. I've lost two members of my family because of him. Things are going to get messy. I want him dead, and I want his hit-man dead. That canister we lifted is my lure ... don't you see? Afterwards, the radioactive stuff is all yours."

Gillian noticed the warmness in his eyes had disappeared. They looked cold, black and empty. The moment reminded her of how she felt the days and weeks after her parents were killed. She couldn't fix what happened. *Accidents are accidents,* she reminded herself, *and sometimes in life you get screwed.*

Gillian filled the awkward silence with a question. "Do you have any suspects?"

He paused for a second. He wondered how beneficial it would be for them to work together. "Have you seen a strange looking woman with the short, spiky hair, oversized glasses, and poorly fitted suits?"

"Yes, Miss Helen Crenshaw. Her boss, Dennis Witherspoon, is in Room 203 recovering from some sort of accident, or surgery, not exactly sure. She's a close talker. Right in your face. A curious and provocative guest. Something's not right with her."

"She keeps some interesting company, namely the businessman with the blonde girlfriend. He has a tribal tat on his forearm designed by my family.

"The blonde girlfriend. Hmm. I guess every man at the hotel has noticed her. Actually they are newlyweds. I met them at the auction. Christine and Brock Hansen. I actually spotted the three of them playing croquet yesterday morning."

"I doubt that's his wife," he added. "Wives are not involved in the family business. At least they weren't when I was around."

"Anyone else?"

"No." The one word response was followed by silence. Harry was notably preoccupied.

"What do you know about the VanBuren family, the grandsons, Ralph and Rem? The ones that ransacked Sol's place, and nailed it with tear gas?" she asked.

"Nothing."

"Do you know why Sol had the birdcage to begin with?"

"No."

Gillian emptied her champagne glass and motioned for a refill. She had to decide whether to bring him up to speed. The tattoo connection he shared was huge. The pieces were falling into place. She sensed it was time to take a leap.

"Sol left me a note. What I found in his safe room, he said, was my insurance. He also warned me strangers would show up asking a lot of questions, and to trust no-one."

"That explains your chilly behavior at our meeting in Fort Myers."

"I had to be. Very clever charade, by the way."

He smiled.

"I know this is a little bizarre, but hear me out. I think the VanBuren's are actually VonBurens, or Von something-or-another, from Brazil. I heard Tilla speak Portuguese the other night at the auction. Why is that important, you ask? Well, I have it on good authority, the Buyer for our birdcage was a terrorist cell out of Germany. I believe a lot of old German money in Brazil could be financing them. The cell doesn't have to be Aryan if they share the same hatred for the good ol' US of A, which makes the Middle Eastern couple interesting, don't you think? You've seen them, right? Homid Patel and his wife, Nadra. She wears a full burka and walks three steps behind him. I get the Sunnis, Shiites mixed up, but maybe they're Hindu." Gillian had begun to ramble.

"Islam split in the 7th Century over who's in charge."

"Huh?" Gillian replied, focused again.

Harry nodded his head but added nothing more. He did notice she referred to the birdcage as *'ours.'*

"What about the oilman from Texas?" she asked.

"I believe he's exactly as he seems: a cowboy."

"The ogre with all the bling," she added.

"He's muscle. Probably someone's messenger."

"Gee, you think? Then there's the recluse, Mr. Witherspoon. No one has actually seen his face. A member of the hotel staff on a room service run tried to snag a quick look, but the man was asleep and his face was covered with bandages. I'm trying to connect the dots here. Maybe he's your Uncle Boris. He's gotten his revenge, but is still looking for his merchandise: the birdcage that Sol escaped with."

"A lot of interesting parties," Harry finally said. His fingers were thumping on the table.

She could picture the wheels turning in his head. "We broker a deal to the highest bidder." Gillian finally said.

"Exactly what I was thinking. Bring him out into the open."

"Glad we agree."

"I can see why my uncle liked you. Do you mind if we take a walk? I need to stretch my legs." He helped her with her chair, and as he did, ran a finger slowly down her back.

Gillian and Harry said good night to the bartender and left the lounge. The main lobby was closed for the evening. The lights were turned down. There was not a soul in sight. The night clerk had placed a sign on the counter saying he would be back in fifteen minutes. As they headed towards the front door, Gillian caught a glimpse of the ogre. He was strolling up the sidewalk, whistling, heading for the front steps. There was nowhere for them to go. The exits were too far away. In a minute they would be totally exposed. For the two of them to be seen together by this guy would jeopardize their plan. She was supposed to be nothing more than a local resident who was clueless as to what was going on. Gillian had to do something. She needed a diversion. The door opened.

Gillian turned to Harry, grabbed him by the lapels

and kissed him with a wanting desire that could not be mistaken. Her lips were soft and voluptuous. Her body leaned seductively into his. She wanted him, there was no mistaking her movement. For Harry, there was but a split hesitation, before his hands were around her waist, pulling her close. Her perfume was intoxicating. Gillian locked her hands around his neck responding in kind to his caressing hands and probing, burning lips. He pushed her back against the wall, shielding her with his body as his hands ran down her well sculptured curves. They were oblivious to their surroundings. He hitched her right leg up and slid his hand up her thigh. A moan slipped from her lips.

The ogre glanced at the two intertwined in the shadows, then walked quickly away. He mumbled under his breath, *"nice piece,"* before he went into the elevator.

The sound of the ding announcing the door was closing signaled to Gillian the coast was clear. She pulled away from Harry's arms, leaving him stunned and confused. He could not downshift that fast.

Gillian cleared her throat. "I think he's gone," she began. "We should probably go before someone else comes."

Harry ran his hands through his hair, straightened his shirt, and adjusted his belt.

"You sure?" he asked. He was definitely not sure of anything at the moment, but held the door for her and followed that nice piece down the steps.

As they made their way to the parking lot, a patrol car pulled in beside them with its blue lights flashing. Gus, Sam's deputy, put the car in park and turned off the engine. He stepped out, along with the Middle Eastern couple, Nadra and Homid Patel, guests from the hotel.

"Miss Gillian, and ... Mr. Stevens, correct?" the deputy asked.

"Yes, that's right."

"Gus, what's this about?"

"This is Agent Amir Dumas and Agent Shirin Feroz from the FBI. They'd like to ask you some questions. If you wouldn't mind getting in the car. I'm to take you over to the station."

Chapter 15

Deputy Gus held open the front door of the police station as Agents Amir Dumas, and Shirin Feroz entered, followed by Gillian and Harry Stevens.

"The sheriff stepped away a little while ago. Reckon he won't care if you use his office. It's right over there." Gus pointed to the room in the far corner.

The foursome piled into the small twelve by twelve foot office. The room was furnished with an old desk and swivel chair, both thin on varnish, three wooden chairs, and a blue tick hound named Beau, who didn't seem interested in staying. Agent Feroz stepped aside to let him out.

The sheriff's desk was empty except for a three line phone, a full cup of coffee, and a partially eaten piece of pecan pie with caramel sauce Lorelei had baked. The dessert was his favorite. Agent Dumas sat behind the desk and felt the mug; barely warm. He had been gone awhile. Agent Feroz closed the blinds, shut the door, then stood by the exit like a sentry at her post. The other two each grabbed a chair and sat down.

Agent Dumas has said nothing up to this point. Being characteristically short on pleasantries, he came straight to the point.

"This is how it's gonna play - a terrorism case involving a murdered witness under federal protection. I believe tampering with evidence and obstruction of justice ought to do the trick."

Gillian shot out of her seat. Harry grabbed the side of the chair before it could tip over.

"Those are trumped up charges, and you know it," she blurted out.

"Sit down," he yelled. His voice reamed with anger. Dumas leaned forward. "Glad to see you're keeping up," he added smugly. "So you understand what this is?"

"It's a frame. Good luck getting it to stick." Gillian pointed out matter-of-factly.

"On the contrary. I have no problem putting some incriminating fingerprints together, along with testimony from the drugged officer on duty. You should appreciate I have a whole litany of anti-terrorism laws at my disposal. I can even cite a public safety exception and hold off reading you your Miranda rights while I enjoy the friendly side of this interrogation."

The arrogance in his voice made her want to slap him.

He continued. "I'm sure you've heard the ongoing debate of how, when and where these cases go to trial. The process is so long and drawn out." He reached over and took a nibble of the pie then licked his fingers. "Incarceration can be so challenging." He turned to Harry. "Good looking guy like yourself, well, you'll be somebody's bitch before the sun sets on your first day inside. As for Miss Crawford, you'll be a punching bag for every white trash prostitute who's got it in for the privileged class like yourself. Your stay won't be pretty."

Harry glanced at Gillian and shook his head. "What do you want?" he asked solemnly.

"We want your uncle, Boris Chenkov, the *Mad Russian.*"

"I haven't seen him."

"We think you have. We know your crime family is here. They came looking for something. Not just to settle a score."

"If you're so familiar with my family, you're aware I've been the estranged nephew for over seventeen years."

"Exactly why the reunion will be all the more sweet."

"I guess this is when you tell us what you have in mind," Gillian said sarcastically.

Agent Feroz stepped up to the desk and laid three 8 x 10 glossies in the middle. The first one she pointed to was VanBuren.

"This man we believe to be Frederick Vanderhauf," Agent Dumas began. Gillian said nothing but felt a tinge of satisfaction. "He and his older brother, Hans, were ten and twelve when their family fled Berlin at the end of the War. Their father was a successful businessman, factories mostly, who was a financial supporter of the Third Reich. The Vanderhauf brothers grew up in Brazil. Privileged childhood, much like you." He glanced Gillian's way. "Hans, the older one, runs things. Frederick follows orders. They seem to still believe in that superior race crap the Germans used to dish out. The brothers recently popped up on our radar. Large amounts of money traced to their family, being moved in and out of a shell corporation added of late to our terrorist watch list. Hans lives in a compound, heavily guarded, in Pomerode, Southern Brazil. One of those settlements, where the vast number of inhabitants are German. Somewhat of a recluse. The brother obviously not so much. Our file on them is a thin one but growing. With Vladimir Polinsky being murdered and Agent Albright, who was his original case officer, found in a ditch with his throat sliced open, well we don't think Frederick is here on holiday."

"So you're saying this Vanderhauf fellow killed my uncle and the Federal Agent? The man's in his early seventies."

Agent Dumas didn't answer. He pointed to the second photograph. "Brock Hansen and wife, Christine. Don't let their corporate facades fool you. We believe they work for your uncle, but we have nothing to pin them with yet. Brock Hansen, aka Andrei Ivanov, has a military background, ex-FSB Special Forces."

"I forget, who's the FSB?" Harry asked.

Dumas seemed perturbed. "Really, Mr. Stevens? They're the new face of the KGB. Ivanov keeps his girlfriend on a short leash. Christine, aka Francesca Arnman, does whatever she's told. Spends most of her time in Switzerland, smurfing Chenkov's dirty money."

"Interesting headshots," Gillian said as she turned to look at Harry. "Who is this?" she asked as she pointed to the last photo.

"This big guy is Yuri Glinka. A bodyguard of sorts. Both brawn and brains. From Chechnya, but doesn't seem to have any Islamic ties. We allow him to travel unimpeded, but follow him with interest. Whatever he does, he's good at covering his tracks.

No outstanding warrants. He has an adjoining room with a Mr. Dennis Witherspoon."

"The recovering businessman whom no one has seen," added Gillian. "Employer to Miss Helen Crenshaw." Gillian couldn't help herself.

"Correct." He seemed unimpressed.

"We believe these are the parties that were transpiring to do business two years ago when Vladimir turned State's evidence. They're back to consummate the transaction. They have fingered you, Miss Crawford, as a person of interest."

"Of which you've had nothing to do with, I'm sure."

"Once we discovered your relationship with Vladimir, we made it possible for them to sniff around your bank accounts, emails, and internet search engines. You've had a sudden drain on your bank and brokerage accounts, I'm afraid. Bad luck at some online gaming sites too. Now they believe you're buying a villa in Tuscany." He paused. Gillian said nothing. The vein in her forehead was now visible. He continued.

"You have an appointment scheduled with a plastic surgeon in London, at the end of the month. A lot of work to be done. Ought to set you back nearly a hundred grand. One would think you have an imminent windfall coming your way. Must have something quite valuable you plan on selling."

"Which is?"

"Why Vladimir's little stash he so cleverly hid from us the first time. Plutonium ore and some uncut diamonds."

"And how would I manage that, since I have

neither?"

"You'll find a package waiting for you back at the hotel's front desk. Should be all you'll need. Don't sell yourself short, Miss Crawford. We know about your association with a Washington think tank called the Zephirine Institute." He didn't wait for a response. "Institute ... well that's not exactly what I'd call it. More like a private club for Langley brainiacs. You're someone who takes care of things. A fixer, thanks to a certain skill set you rather enjoy. You're well-schooled. Seems like a logical assumption you'll figure something out. It's what you're good at, isn't it? You've got 24 hours." He looked at his wristwatch. "Tick-tock."

As Harry and Gillian stood up to leave, she reached out for the photographs on the desk but tipped the coffee cup over instead. Agent Dumas wasn't quick enough. The cup of joe splattered all over his pants. His crotch was soaked. Gillian followed Harry out and slammed the door behind them. Beau, the blue tick hound, bolted to the office door and growled.

Harry grabbed Gillian by the arm as they headed outside.

"You're a part of this? You work for these people?" He was livid.

She shook him off. "I never worked for the Bureau. And I'm pretty sure, Agents Dumas and Feroz don't either."

"I think you're all part of the intelligence community. You fabricate, spin and promote fear to justify your existence."

"Not anymore," Gillian replied. "Let's walk back

to the hotel. I'll tell you what I can."

The return trip was six blocks. Gillian gazed up at the sky and took a deep breath. What an amazing view. No bright, city lights to blur out the stars. In her mind, she was reeling off names of constellations. She was going to miss this too. *Damn you, Boris Chenkov*, she swore to herself.

"I was attending Queen's College at Oxford when they first approached me. Philosophy, of all things, but I enjoyed the subject. Not a real demand for Philosophers in the workplace though. They made an interesting argument for doing something useful and valuable with my life."

"Who exactly is *'they'*?"

"Yeah ... that's not happening. The name of the think tank Dumas mentioned, that sounds good. We'll go with that."

"But now you're out?"

"Couple years ago, I got a call. I was in ... well, Lebanon, actually. There was an accident. Both my parents were killed. They had just purchased a 54 foot sedan bridge and were cruising back from Key West. The public story was a leak in the fuel line caused an explosion. What really happened, was they were coming back late at night, and were spotted by a drug runner. Rotten luck. Wrong place, wrong time. The Coast Guard recovered some crucial evidence in the wreckage; evidence tied to an ongoing investigation they didn't want released to the public. A bigger fish to fry they said. So that's the story we ran with."

"I'm sorry."

"I lost my focus afterwards. My employer granted

me a sabbatical, which was very generous. But in their eyes, it meant I was out."

"Not sure I buy that," Harry responded. He was skeptic by default. "I have a lot of unanswered questions and doubts at the moment." His irritation had calmed a bit, but not much. "And if those Agents aren't FBI, then who are they? Plus, what's this about diamonds. Have you seen those? Because I sure the hell haven't."

She shook her head. "I need to hurry back to the hotel and see what this package is. I have no intention of being framed and put in prison. I've no more get-out-of-jail free cards. No favors to call in."

By now they had made it to the fringes of the hotel parking lot. Harry stood close to her and peered down at her face. Her green eyes were dark and brimming with hate. "What, so now you have a plan?" he asked.

"Sort of. Meet me back here tomorrow night around ten. I've got some personal things I need to take care of. I suggest you be ready to move on a moment's notice. Ever hear of a go-bag?" Gillian didn't wait for a reply"

BACK AT THE station, Gus was pouring himself a cup of coffee when the sheriff returned. "You just missed them," he said.

"Missed who?" the sheriff asked.

"Those FBI Agents. Dumas and Feroz."

"What are you talking about?"

"Agent Amir Dumas and, what's her name, Agent ... Shirin Feroz. They wanted to speak with Miss Gillian, and a fella by the name of Harry Stevens, that's staying over at the hotel. I drove on over, got them, and brought them back here. They all went into your office for about fifteen minutes, then left. None of them seemed happy, that's for sure."

"And where are they now?"

"Don't know. They didn't say."

The sheriff went over to his desk and unlocked his lap drawer. He pulled out a fax he had received earlier from the FBI advising him of the arrival of Agents Simon Beck and Ruth Ross in the morning. He picked up his phone, dialed the number and extension on the letterhead. It went straight to an automatic script with a ten minute wait time. "Damnit," he growled and slammed down the receiver. He then picked up his cold piece of pie, threw it in the trashcan, and headed out the door.

Chapter 16

"Hadley, it's me," Gillian began. "Sorry to call so late. We need to talk. Mind if I come over?"

"Sounds serious."

"Might be if things don't go well."

"All right. Come in the back door. No sense broadcasting your visit."

Hadley lived in one of the cottages located on the west side of the hotel. Seven units, six for rent. Pastel colored, Key West style. Deep front porches, abundant palms, bamboo floors, and well stocked mini-bars. His was #7, farthest from the main building, making for less noise and foot traffic.

By the time Gillian arrived, Hadley had turned off the lights. She entered through the rear of his one bedroom cottage and quietly shut the back screened door. Hadley stood in the hallway to greet her.

"How about some of that Scotch you're always bragging about," she added.

Hadley walked over to the liquor cabinet and grabbed an unopened bottle of 18 year old single-malt. "So, you made it out of Sol's cottage in one piece. Find anything worth killing for, missy?" Hadley's matter-of-fact comment was actually designed to cultivate her confidence. Inwardly, he had become a mother hen.

"A girl's best friend. Large. A variety of cut and uncut. Pink, yellow and white. Enough to finance a sizable arms deal, or an ugly dirty bomb."

"That'll do," he said.

"Wait, there's more," she attempted to smile, sounding like an infomercial. "I also found what every terrorist on the planet would love to get their hands on."

"No way. Behind the old man's fireplace? Hold on, how secure is the material?"

"I dropped the birdcage off at Father Flannigan's about three hours ago, and yes, the ore has been properly contained. He's not privy to what's inside. I asked him to stay clear of it. Told him I'd be back to pick up the package in a day or two. The diamonds are right here." She held her black clutch purse over the kitchen table and turned the latch to the left. A false bottom compartment popped open, and they slid out on the countertop.

Hadley picked up a pink one, twirled the jewel in his fingers and whistled. "Well, aren't you pretty. How much you suppose?"

"Fifty mill, maybe more. Pink ones that size are pretty rare. Who do we know in the business capable of handling a load this size?"

"Remember the guy in Brussels we used a few years ago for that smoke and mirrors operation? Christophe Wiseman. But he's going to ask for a significant cut." Gillian made a mental note.

Hadley changed the subject. "Did you figure out who the guys were that stormed the old man's place?"

"Brazilian by address. German by descent. At least that's what two government agents, purporting to be from the Bureau, told me."

Hadley held his glass in midair, surprised by what she said. "Can't be too many Nazi sympathizers still alive."

"Second and third generation, I'm afraid. Old money still making political turmoil."

"What does the Bureau think?"

"Remember those plans for rainy days you schooled me on?"

Hadley turned towards her with a troubled brow.

"Well, as luck would have it, a torrential one is coming my way. His name is Agent Dumas, and he's threatening me with trumped up charges if I don't help him find a Russian mobster they've lost track of. Nickname, the *Mad Russian*. Most likely responsible for Sol's murder. Family feud. The ore belonged to the Russians, and the diamonds to the Brazilians." She was trying to sound calm, but inside she was trembling.

"Wait, the Agent is or is not with the FBI?"

"Not FBI."

"Who then?"

"Mossad."

He choked on his scotch. "Excuse me. Israeli Intelligence here on the island. They can't frame you. Tell 'em to go screw themselves."

"I'd love to, but later. Right now I've got something else in mind."

"They don't realize you're in possession of these?"

Gillian shook her head.

"How do they expect you to seem legit without the diamonds?"

"They've provided me with the means."

"What does that mean?"

Gillian tried to sound optimistic. "Actually, they're pretty decent fakes."

"How much time do we have?"

"Less than 24 hours. As for you, that's what I wanted to talk with you about." She finished off her scotch, slowly laid the glass on the counter, and took a slow, deep breath. What she was about to say, was tough, with difficult ramifications.

"I don't know what kind of arrangement you and Uncle Jack have, but seriously, Hadley, you need to let go and live your own life. I can do this. I'm ready to do this."

"Forget your uncle, just tell me what I can do to help."

She studied him for a moment and smiled bleakly. "Okay, well first off, here's the legal stuff. This should be everything you need." She handed him a black leather portfolio. "The house keys, offshore bank accounts and pin. The local stuff they've already gotten to. Here's my Will and Power of Attorney. Do whatever you feel is best with the house, cars and boat. Like I said, Father Flannigan has the glow-in-the-dark stuff. What I have for the diamond dealer, Wiseman, will be hanging up in Willie Ray's workshop. If you could handle the shipment. I have a decoy going to Uncle Jack's place in Florence, just in case. Promise me you'll find Ollie a good home, and remember, I'm fond of daisies."

He nodded. "What's next?"

"I need you to bring back Sol's sailboat to the marina and set up a booby trap."

"You found his boat, where?"

"Pretty sure at Useppa Island. But go off island by car and take the water taxi. You'll need to make some minor cosmetic changes to her name. They're monitoring the marina.

"And the booby trap, what did you have in mind?"

"Enough to destroy the sailboat and whoever comes calling."

"What else?"

"I need a diversion here at the hotel. The incident needs to be significant. Has to be believable. Life threatening, in fact. Something that will bring all the guests out of the woodwork. Every last one of them. I need the hotel evacuated and empty for an hour with no intrusions."

"When?"

"Ten, tomorrow night."

"Anything else?"

"One last thing. Remember your friend from the wildlife refuge south of town?"

"Yes, but what could you possibly need from the zoo?"

"One of your little friends."

He rolled his eyes. "Can't you pick something else?"

"One small, colorful one."

"Those are the worst kind."

"Exactly why they'll fit the bill."

Hadley sighed and shook his head. "Of all the things in our arsenal, you choose that? Are you sure?"

"Have your guy milk it and deliver both to my room. Honestly, you're such a lightweight."

"Lightweight. Really? I'll have you know, caution is synonymous with wisdom, which comes with age."

"You've got me there."

"You're familiar with the pre-frontal cortex of your brain which controls rational behavior?"

"I've studied the various sections of the brain, yes" she replied, with all the servility she could muster.

Hadley tapped his finger on her forehead. "But are you aware the cortex does not fully develop until your twenty five. And in some, it's delayed."

"Thank you, Dr. Freud." Gillian was trying to make light of the situation before she had to leave. There were to be no goodbyes. A rule established long ago. Hadley handed her another glass of courage, and they toasted to the uncertain future.

"I suppose if you're going to leave the nest, I need to equip you properly. Let's see what I can do on short notice." Hadley walked over to his double oven, turned both top and bottom dials to Broil, then waited for a click. The unit rolled out from the wall, and he pushed the appliance aside.

"A hidden closet, really? Crandle must be the go to guy on the island," she chuckled. Hadley shook his head and grinned. Gillian had to stand on her tiptoes to see over his shoulder. He grabbed a handful of items and placed them on the kitchen table.

"Okay, since it's been a while, here's a quick refresher course." He proceeded to point to each one.

"Tire slasher. Sharp hook. Old school, but the razor-edge blade does the trick."

Gillian eased her finger over the blade.

"Next, a spy camera."

"They still make those things?"

"Upgraded. Everything's digital. Handy for close up work. Fits in the palm of your hand. See?"

Gillian grabbed the tiny camera and took a quick shot of his face. He rolled his eyes.

"This is a Fiberscope. Connect the USB to your laptop or tablet, goes under the door, you get audio and video. Heads up on curious pets."

"Watch out for Fido." She nodded her head.

"Next, another old school item: three finger grip push dagger. Effective because the weapon is forceful at close range. I won't demonstrate."

"Colossal force at close range. Got it."

He reached for the next item and hesitated. "This is an intradermal punch needle filled with a dose of ... Hydrogen Cyanide. You pretend to accidentally bump into your assailant as you punch it, then walk away. The poison works fast, and its lethal."

Gillian eyed the needle carefully. "Don't remember that one." Her expression was grim. Hadley's too.

Next, he picked up a listening device. "Looks like another bug," Gillian said.

"This one works with a cone. Twenty times more powerful than the others. It's in case you need to eavesdrop from a second story window, on a conversation at street level. May come in handy."

"Or at least entertaining."

"I had some passports made for us before we left. They're clean. Remember the little stuff as you create your new identity. Pocket litter, for instance. Receipts, used bus passes, ticket stubs, that sort of thing."

Hadley reached for the last item, a flash drive. This is loaded with encryption software, including digital steganography for hiding messages. That's steganography, not stenography, by the way. Use the e-mail account I set up for us, back in the day. You still remember the password?"

"Yep."

"Bear in mind you never send or receive anything to this account. We communicate only by reading the unsent drafts. Keep them simple. Hide the message within a scenic photograph, like a colorful flower, or a busy street, using this software program. All right?"

"I don't know what to say, Santa. I feel like it's Christmas."

"While we're tying up loose ends, you honestly don't know what your uncle's offer was?"

"Not a clue," she replied.

Hadley hesitated. "Sealed files for both of us. No retribution for the past. I like to sleep well at night, so I took him up on his offer. He realized being your uncle and closest of kin, he wasn't cut out to be the guardian type. Guess he figured you'd get yourself into hot water occasionally," he raised his eyebrows and nodded his head, "so, he set me up here. All in all, not a bad gig. Remember the operation we ran in Kashmir, when the Minister of Foreign Affairs needed a last minute chef for a lavish party?"

"I remember your bananas Foster singed the invited dignitary's beard."

"Albeit, that training came in handy."

"I knew Uncle Jack had influence, but not that much." She shook her head.

"So if everything goes as planned, which I know it will, where are you headed?"

"I'll let you know when I'm settled." Her smile was guarded this time.

He kissed her affectionately on the top of the head, just as Father Flannigan did, and watched her walk away; wondering what the next forty-eight hours would bring. In the many years he had been in the business, she was the sharpest rookie he had ever recruited.

BROCK HANSEN STOOD at the window of his third floor hotel room facing the front steps, and speed dialed a number on his cell phone.

"She's back from the police station. Doesn't look too happy."

"Is she alone?" asked the raspy Russian voice on the other end.

"Yep. That guy she was with, that goes by the name Stevens, is nowhere in sight. I did a little background check on him. Not much there. And I don't mean run of the mill, not much there. I mean it only went back a few years. We believe his real name is Cantore. Runs a little export company out of Naples. You said he looked familiar?"

"Possibly."

"What do you want us to do?"

"I'll keep an eye on him. You stay close to the Crawford woman."

"All right. So what do you make of the police roundup?"

"They want us to think she's working for them. Maybe she's been persuaded to. She'll need to make contact with us. They'll have her on a short leash. You and Francesca make yourself approachable. Drop a hint big enough for her to trip over. Let me know when she makes the initial contact."

BACK INSIDE HER hotel room, Gillian stood

next to the desk looking at the clever substitute for uncut diamonds. The small cylinder, however, filled with what seemed like a chiseled down version of charcoal with a tinge of yellow powder, was a joke. In her hand was the business card Father Francis passed on to her - the exporter down in Naples. Cantore. Italian. She flipped the card over several times in her hands. There was an idea worth perusing. She looked at her watch. She'd call in the morning. Gillian grabbed a sheet of hotel stationery and scribbled a note to her new Italian acquaintances, Pauly and Renzo, asking them if they wanted to join her for breakfast down at the marina. Gillian rang the front desk, and a hotel staff member from the night shift arrived a few minutes later to pick up the note and deliver it.

Gillian needed to get some rest. It would be her last chance for the next two days. She set her alarm for six and drifted off to sleep.

Chapter 17

The marina was the island's quintessential public place to meet. Being out in the open, all eyes and ears could take notice of what Gillian was up to, even at seven o'clock in the morning. If you fished, you were up at the crack of dawn. The hotel had packed her a basket including a thermos of coffee, Canadian bacon, egg and cheese breakfast sandwiches, and fruit. She told them to forget the yogurt.

Gillian, Pauly and Renzo had breakfast at one of the weather worn picnic tables located by the main pier. Renzo inhaled his then headed with coffee in hand to their boat, docked temporarily by the diesel pumps.

"A handwritten note, smelling of perfume, delivered after midnight is a bit suspicious. But when a beautiful lady like yourself offers me breakfast, I'm all in. So whazzup? Band of pirates on the loose or something?"

"Well, to be perfectly honest, I find myself in need of unloading a highly marketable commodity in a hurry, and wondered if you could put me in contact with someone you trust."

Pauly turned serious, checked his surroundings for anyone in earshot, and studied her face. He took a sip of his coffee and cleared his throat. "Can you be a bit more specific?"

"Diamonds, most are uncut, untraceable. Eight figures. Tomorrow at the latest. There's a one percent finder's fee for you and Renzo."

He whistled softly. "Aren't you full of surprises. Okay. Let me make a call. I'll get back with you later this morning." He grabbed his cell phone and got up from the table. "Thanks for breakfast, sweetheart."

Agent Shirin Feroz, sitting in a black unmarked sedan in the gravel parking lot, contacted her partner, Amir. "She's started to make her move."

"Excellent."

"Someone else is watching her too."

"Who?"

"Looks like the Chechnyan."

"Stick with him, but don't get too close."

SAM MITCHELL ENTERED the police station at eight a.m. Lorelei was already at work. A fresh pot of coffee had just finished brewing. He walked by the fax machine and pulled off two pages from the hopper: the FBI alert containing the coroner's report on Philip Albright, the dead Agent, pulled out of the ditch. Sam poured himself a cup of coffee and sat down in his swivel chair.

The Alert at the top read, "Fingerprints and DNA of deceased are not a match to Agent Philip Albright. Deceased identified through CODIS as Simon Cantore. Last address of record: Tamiami Trail NE, Naples, Florida. Occupation: Export Agent. Whereabouts of Agent Albright unknown.

Sam Mitchell gulped down his coffee. Someone had gone to a lot of trouble to fake that identity. Badge, money, airplane tickets, itinerary. Why had this agent disappeared, and where did he go? He grabbed the file for Solomon Crawford and flipped through the report. Albright had been his original case officer the first year he went into the system.

"Lorelei," the sheriff snapped. "I need the badge photo on file for Agent Albright. Get the Bureau on the phone. See if you can get me one pronto."

"He's not with the Bureau. Don't you remember, he worked for the U.S. Marshal's Service?"

"I don't give a rat's ass where he worked, just get me his photo on the double."

Lorelei bit her lip. Her eyes welled up with tears. All feelings aside, his verbal dumping was getting old. Next time she baked him a pie, she swore she would spit in it.

GILLIAN WAS SITTING in the hotel's salon enjoying a pleasant conversation with Christine Hansen when the text message arrived from Pauly. At first she ignored it.

"I love your engagement ring," she said, nodding to it lying on the table. "Your husband has exquisite taste. That is simply gorgeous."

"He's a keeper," she said with a smile. They were both having mani-pedis. Gillian had finished but was inspecting her toes. Christine Hansen's hands were still under the console dryer.

Gillian glanced down quickly at the phone, blocking it from Christine's view. *"Noon. Fountain at City Hall Complex, Fort Myers. Blue linen shirt. Floral design. White Pants. Name is Finn."*

"Oh good," Gillian began. "Looks like I got a t-time after all." She glanced at the clock on the wall. The location was an hour away, if she flew. At least her mafia connection had picked a public place. It seemed to be a day of visiting public places. She had a gnawing feeling in the pit of her stomach. This Finn guy better be sharp. The next few days could be unpleasant for both of them.

"I guess I'd better go grab my clubs. I don't know what your plans are Christine, or how long you're staying, but the hotel hosts an art class once a month, sponsored by the local art league. It's tomorrow evening. The gathering is more of an excuse to drink wine, but we do dabble with paint. They provide all the materials and supplies. A particular painting from a famous artist is selected, and one of the locals provide instruction, helping us with our own interpretation, each step of the way. I think this month we're doing one of Tarkay's - an amazing artist. You never know what hidden talent is among us. A diamond in the rough, so to speak," she chuckled. "If you're free, you should come."

"Sounds interesting. I'll try. Thank you."

"Oh, and don't forget to put your ring back on. You'd be surprised how many women forget, and call the salon in a panic."

Gillian went back to her uncle's suite, called the front desk, and asked for a bell boy ASAP. She glanced around her hotel suite and picked out two of the most ornate paintings on the wall. Uncle Jack's staff had the most dreadful taste in art, let alone frames. They seemed to think anything large and bodacious qualified as fine art. She pulled a couple off the wall and sat them down by the door. A few minutes later, Enrique arrived. Again with the smile, she thought. *Is that all teenage boys think about,* she wondered?

"I need for you to run a little errand for me.

Here's a hundred. Go to the hardware store down on Pelican Street. Get me a bottle of Elmer's glue and a spray can of gold paint. Better get two. Make sure, and I mean absolutely sure, you buy latex. If it's not in stock, go over to the mainland and get some. Just be quick about it. I'll be back in about three hours. Take what you purchase, as well as these paintings, to the grounds keeper's shed. If Willie Ray is working, tell him I'll be by for them later. You can keep the change. Got it?"

"Yes ma'am. I'll take care of everything. I'm eager to assist you any way I can. Call me day or night."

She shook her head and chuckled. "Scoot! Now," and waved him out the door.

Gillian grabbed her cell phone and looked at the to-do list she had compiled before going to sleep. She picked up the business card, Father Francis had given her and dialed the number on the back. The call rang twice before the other party picked up.

"Yes, is this Simon Cantore? Your business card was given to me by a mutual friend, Solomon Crawford."

"It is." The voice on the other end sounded guarded.

Gillian hesitated when she heard him speak, but continued. "My name is Gillian Crawford. No relation."

"What can I help you with, ma'am?"

Again she hesitated, but this time she was sure. "Harry?"

There was silence on the other end.

"Harry, I know that's you."

"Call me back when you can secure the line," he whispered. Click went the connection.

"I don't have time for this," she moaned out loud. "Let me just whip out a freakin' satellite phone from my hip pocket and call you back, Simon Cantore, I mean Harry Stevens, or are you Max Taylor. Jeez. Who the bloody hell are you?"

Frustrated and short on time, Gillian changed into a bright colored sundress with pink sandals, evoking a touristy look, before stopping by the kitchen to visit with Hadley.

"You didn't come by for breakfast."

"Had mine bright and early over at the marina. I've gotta run to Fort Myers. Be back in a few hours. I'm here to borrow that GPS tracking device I pulled off my car. I want to be sure certain people know exactly where I am, and where I'm headed."

"That's a first. I wasn't able to pull any info off of it, sorry. It's a generic model. Tens of thousands sold." Hadley shook his head and continued to slice up some strawberries.

"You still have that satellite phone you took as a parting gift?"

"Why yes, I do," he smiled. "I'm guessing on the flip side you don't want Big Brother listening."

"Right," she replied.

"I can arrange that. Three hours, you say?"

"Yes. I should be back by then."

"I'm leaving in a few minutes myself, to take care of those errands we talked about earlier."

"Oh good, thanks." She started to leave, but turned and said, "What am I going to do without you?"

"We'll think of something. I could use a change of scenery too."

THE FOUNTAIN AT the Judicial Complex in Fort Myers was a popular midday spot for tourist as well as professionals on their smoke or lunch break. It was also frequently vandalized by adolescent pranksters administering liquid soap to the water source.

Gillian parked her car down the side street and walked slowly around the perimeter before heading to the fountain. A few minutes before noon a middle aged man, jet black hair, deep tan, left hand cupping a cigarette, walked nonchalantly to the fountain and flipped a coin in the water. He was dressed in the described blue shirt, and white pants, looking like a regular guest at the Fontainebleau on Collins Avenue.

Gillian walked up to him and introduced herself.

"Thank you for meeting me on such short notice."

"Yeah, no problem. Pauly and Renzo speak real highly of you."

"I'll get straight to the point. Delivery will be tomorrow night. I'll be in a hurry and may be followed, so be prepared. They're pink, yellow and white stones. Most are uncut, untraceable and decent in size. Don't suppose you care one way or another if their conflict diamonds. I believe they're from Brazil though. Forty pink, twenty yellow, the remainder, white. The majority of the colored ones are each over three carats. Here's a sample." Gillian handed him a small, white linen handkerchief.

Fifty yards away, a black Escalade pulled up to the curb. The limo-tint front window went down.

Yuri spotted Gillian handing a white handkerchief to a guy dressed in a blue shirt. He took something out of the cloth and held it up to the sun. The object sparkled. Yuri flipped open his phone.

"We got her. She's meeting with the fence right now. I'll follow him. You're still tracking her, right?"

"Yes, I've got her," answered Nikolay. His fingers were flying over the keyboard.

Finn glanced around the fountain looking for anything out of the ordinary. "This big, this fast, I can only do thirty cents on the dollar."

"Really? Pauly led me to believe you could handle this."

Finn rubbed the whiskers on his face and sighed. "All right. Forty. But I'm only interested in the uncut ones."

"Sixty," she shot back.

"Lady, no one gets sixty anymore."

"All right, we'll split it down the middle. And you can keep that one."

"Deal." They shook hands. Gillian felt like she needed a shower.

"Oh, and Pauly and Renzo get one percent, of which we split," she added.

"Yeah, I already heard. They'll be close by. So where do we meet?" he asked.

"Tomorrow night at 9:45 p.m. Eighteenth green, Boca Grande Hotel golf course."

"Text me thirty minutes before, so I know we're still on."

"Thank you, Mr. Finn. Pleasure doing business with you."

"Likewise, lady. Thanks for the tip. And it's just

Finn."

"Okay, Just Finn."

Chapter 18

Finn Giordano pulled his shiny, black Lincoln Towncar into the reserved parking lot at the Ft. Myers Yacht Basin. Slip owners had designated parking. He grabbed a six pack of Peroni and headed to his sixty-four foot cruiser he called home: *Il Mio Amore.* His mind was preoccupied; mulling over the pending transaction with the Boca dame and her diamonds. A thin margin, but the profit would set him up nicely. He'd go from semi-retired to no worries in a heartbeat. After the quality of goods was verified, the money would move quickly. Payment was all electronic these days. Off-shore bank accounts, passwords, PINS, fingerprint scans. He entered the galley kitchen and parked the six pack in the refrigerator.

Finn had lived on his yacht for two years, moving back and forth from the east and west coast of Florida as boredom would dictate. He was familiar with every creak and sound his boat made. There was nothing silent about someone walking up on deck when you were down below. He reached over and pulled his gun out of the microwave. A Glock with a full clip and a custom made silencer. What kind of enemies did this Crawford chick have? He flipped off the safety, dialed Pauly's cell and turned around. He heard Pauly pick up.

Two hits from the metal baseball bat put Finn on his knees. The guy was quick. A jab to his lower gut, followed by a whack to his knee caps. Finn's cell phone slid under the Galley kitchen cabinet.

"Unless you want more, you'd better start talking," growled Yuri Glinka.

Finn managed to peer up at his assailant and spit a mouthful of blood on the guy's shoes. He must have been 6'5" and weighed three hundred pounds.

The insult from Finn drew another hit, this time to his lower back. Finn rolled over on his side and squeezed off a shot, barely missing the guy's thigh. Glinka knocked the weapon away, then whacked the Italian's hand with the bat. The skin over his smashed knuckles busted opened, with blood spattering everywhere.

"All right, all right," he pleaded. "What do ... you want?"

"My boss wants to know when and where's the Crawford drop?"

Finn was keenly aware his time was up. He had looked over his shoulder his entire life. Apprehension came with the territory. Here he was, about to enjoy a new chapter in his life. The irony. But at least he would screw this bastard from the grave.

"Tomorrow night. 9:45 p.m. Boca Grande Hotel golf course. Eighteenth green."

Not another word was spoken. Yuri reached down and picked up the pistol. The silencer kept it private. Two to the chest and one to the head. Finn gasped for air, stiffened, then collapsed on the floor. He slowly bled out.

Yuri reached down, frisked his pockets and found the white linen handkerchief the Crawford dame gave him earlier. He opened the cloth and found an uncut stone. White. About two carats, he'd guess. The diamond went into his pocket. At the back of the yacht, he found a red fuel can and dumped gasoline over the salon and galley floors. He then emptied the remaining bullets from the clip, put them in the microwave and set the timer for ten minutes. He was two miles away before the blast went off.

PAULY STOOD SILENTLY on the pier next to the Boca Grande Marina listening on his cell phone to the whack job going down in Ft. Myers. His face was red, beet red. He was sixty miles away and could do nothing. Finn, who was thirty years his senior was a member of the Family. He moved to South Florida when he turned 60 to live a less hectic life. Now he was lying dead on the floor *of Il Mio Amore*, the victim of a professional hit. Finn was aware Pauly was on the line when he tossed the phone; otherwise he would have never given up those specifics. Finn knew the Family would settle this. Pauly called an unlisted phone number in Nevada. The vacation was over.

GILLIAN RETURNED TO the hotel around four o'clock and poked her head inside the kitchen. Hadley glanced over, shouted out, "Nice stripes," and pointed to the ceiling. She guessed that meant everything was upstairs in Uncle Jack's suite.

On her way back from Ft. Myers, Gillian bought three burn phones. Before using the first one, she placed a call from the wide open landline to Uncle Jack's assistant, Claudia, who was in charge of the auction.

"I noticed we have quite a few purchases we need

to ship internationally this year. I have a new shipping company I'd like to use. Cantore Exports. They're out of Naples. She glanced at the business card in her hand. "Their tag line is, *'We beat any competitor by 20%.'* I'll text their phone number to you. Would you give them a call? I'd like to have them pick up everything tomorrow afternoon, if possible."

"Sure. I'd be happy to. Did you not like the company we used last year?"

"They were okay. Someone told me this company was great to deal with, and with their advertised discount, I thought we'd give them a try. Make a little profit on the shipping and handling we quoted so we could pass the savings on to the orphanage fund."

"Great idea. I'll give them a call right now."

"Oh, and Claudia, I have one of Uncle Jack's I'll be shipping too. I'll have the painting at the delivery door in a couple of hours. The shipping info will be taped to the back: it's going to his home in Tuscany."

"I'll see to the shipment personally. Glad the auction turned out well. Your uncle called earlier this morning and wanted to talk with you. I gave him the preliminary numbers. He wants you to give him a call as soon as possible."

Gillian glanced at her watch and rolled her eyes. "I will. Thanks.

DOWN ON THE second floor in a junior suite was Harry Stevens. The door was locked from the inside, and a chair was wedged under the door handle for extra security. He was sitting at a desk working on a laptop, with earbuds in. He had tapped into the hotel's phone system and had listened to Gillian's conversation with her uncle's secretary. She was clever, he'd give her that. He would need to intercept her uncle's crate and inspect the contents

GILLIAN GRABBED HER clutch purse with the fake bottom on her way to the golf shed. "Willie Ray, are you here?" Gillian yelled as she entered the dark green wooden golf and mechanical shed along the back side of the hotel's property line. The jalousie windows were open marginally. The air inside smelled of grease and fertilizer. Overhead the fluorescent lights buzzed and flickered. In the corner was a small portable radio, set to a Gospel station, playing, 'Oh, Happy Day.' It was one of those songs that would stick in your head. She spotted a handwritten note on the bench saying, he was out on the back nine, and would return in about an hour. Gillian took a gander around the inside. Enrique had laid a plastic bag from the hardware store on the work bench and placed the two paintings against it.

Gillian grabbed yesterday's newspaper from the bench, spread out a half dozen pages on the ground and got busy.

An hour later, she threw the makeshift drop cloth in the trash can, stood back and looked at her work. One of the two paintings was now hung up on the back wall overlooking the utility sink. The painting of an old man and his donkey, outside the Partagas cigar factory in Cuba, was now embellished with an ornate, gold frame. The other painting of a border collie herding sheep, also adorned in gold, was propped up at the door, with a note attached: *ship to*

Jonathan Cromwell's home in Florence, Italy.

As she made her way back to the front entrance of the hotel, Sam Mitchell pulled in under the portico and got out. He stood by the dark gray, unmarked car and motioned with his index finger for her to come over.

Gillian could tell by the look on his face, this was not going to be pleasant.

"Gus tells me you were brought in for questioning last night, by the FBI."

"Is that a question?"

"You all right?"

"I've been better."

"Care to fill me in?"

"Didn't they fill you in already?" Sam detected a clear annoyance in her tone.

He glared at her but said nothing.

"Let's go for a walk," she said. "I feel like getting some fresh air."

The two of them headed away from the hotel, down a quiet, Banyon canopy street that led to the old mission house.

He remained silent as he walked close by her side. She reached out for his hand as they continued towards the end of the street.

"I never told you how I met Hadley, did I?"

"No, can't say you have."

"I met him before he was gainfully employed as a chef."

"Really?"

"Yes, when I was at Oxford. He offered me a job, but meaningful employment was not what I was looking for. You know me, easily bored, an odd creature, I might as well say it because everyone thinks so, plus, I've never been great at embracing the average day to day."

"That's one way to put it," he grinned.

"For six years I worked for a think tank, which was affiliated with ... well let's just say we did some specialty work for an intelligence agency. Sometimes it's a good idea to run a parallel agenda, in case the sanctioned one doesn't go well."

"You were a ... ."

"Yes." She stopped walking after giving a one word answer, looked at him and nodded her head. He dropped her hand.

"We don't use that term anymore. Post Cold-War. Asset is the modern sobriquet."

"Hadley too then?"

"My handler. He taught me everything I know. I was lucky he took me under his wing. Teacher. Mentor. Whatever the label is these days. He was big into the Socratic Method. Questions, answers, more questions, more answers. Inquiry and debate. He would find holes in my thought process and make me rethink things. Find an alternate means. When I'd get stumped, or run into a brick wall, he would ask, "If someone had a gun to your head, and you had to get something done, what would you do; how would you figure it out?" That line of thinking helped a lot when it came to, shall we say, analyze situations and circumstances in real time. When I spouted off, *'I'm not some helpless, little female,'* well now you know why."

"Why are you telling me this now? Does it have anything to do with your late night meeting in my office with the FBI?"

"Are you sure they're with the Bureau?" she asked.

"Hmm. You have doubts? Why?"

"Blackmail for one. Pretty sure they're with a foreign intelligence agency though. Very well informed."

"The real agents, Simon Beck and Ruth Ross, arrived this morning. So now are you going to tell me about your little meeting?"

"Amir Dumas, Agent for ... gee, I don't know, take your pick, and yes I'm profiling, found out I used to work for a think tank. He's speculating on the job description. He's using some trumped up charges as leverage, so he thinks. He also discovered that Harry Stevens is Sol Crawford's nephew."

"Who is Harry Stevens?"

"Oh, I guess you don't know him. Well, he's a guest here at the hotel. Sol, who's true name was Vladimir Polinsky absconded with a butt load of diamonds and radioactive material, enough for a dirty bomb. Dumas seems to think we can bring some interested parties out in the open, who would like to buy the commodities, namely a Russian Mafia figure with the moniker, the *Mad Russian*, who apparently is Harry Steven's other uncle, and a Jew hater by the name of Vanderhauf. So I guess you can figure out which one they're after."

"Vanderhauf."

"Yep."

"Mossad."

"I believe so. You do realize that's not some urban legend about their little band of helpers. It's the Sayanim register. Local Jewish communities have a list of volunteers that help out when required. If someone needs to know the comings and goings of the police staff on the island, well I'm sure somebody came forward and helped them. Why did you leave last night, by the way."

"Call on the hotline about someone looking suspicious by the bridge, but the tip didn't pan out."

"See? They orchestrated you being elsewhere, knowing that Gus would assume they were whom they said they were. Anyway, if all goes as planned the meeting is to take place tonight at the hotel around ten o'clock."

"You have these items to trade?"

"Well, obviously not. It's why Amir's counting on me pulling a rabbit out of a hat."

"And you're sharing this with me now because ... why?"

"I thought you might want to be close by, in case things go sour. But not too close. We don't want to spook them. It's all conjecture at this point. Can't prove anything quite yet."

"Hadley's been told?"

"Yes, and you might want to pay Father Flannigan a visit in a day or two."

"So this Harry Stevens guy is Russian?"

"Yes. Changed his name, changed his life. Got out of the family business when he was a teenager. He is, by the way, Max Taylor, from Sol's encrypted newspaper message."

"A lot of aliases."

At this point, Gillian's mind was drifting off. "As well as Simon Cantore," she added softly.

Sam reached over to her and grabbed her shoulders. "That wouldn't be Simon Cantore from Naples, Florida, in the export business would it?"

Gillian looked at him guardedly then answered, "Yes. Why?"

"That was his body we pulled out of the ditch two days ago."

"Wait. I thought he was Federal Agent Philip Albright?" Gillian felt as if she'd been punched in the stomach.

"Afraid not."

"Well, that changes everything."

"What do you mean?"

"Means I need to go." She started to turn but stopped. If ever there was a time for a fond farewell, this was it. Gillian leaned over and kissed him. Torrid, passionate, unforgettable. She made sure it was all there.

"I'll see you tomorrow," she whispered to him, held his face in her hands, then turned and walked away.

Sam watched her leave. She raised her arm and waved. He called out, "Gillian, wait up."

She kept going, but yelled over her shoulder, "I'll see you tomorrow." A lone tear ran down her cheek.

Chapter 19

*O*ut and About was a once a month island celebration, sponsored by the local merchants, held the second Wednesday of each month from five o'clock until the beer ran out. The downtown area, an eight block section, would come alive with local troubadours, fresh seafood to savor, and plenty of cold brew to wash it down.

There was no better place to make oneself visible than at the corner of Gasper and Main. Christine and Brock Hansen strolled that direction with mojitos in hand. He motioned to his wife when he spotted Gillian Crawford walking along the street towards them. Christine stopped at the corner to listen to a reggae band jamming as he continued on.

Hansen walked directly in Gillian's path and dropped his keys. He stopped. She stopped. He had blocked her way.

"I represent an interested party who would like to do business with you, Miss Crawford."

Dumas's glossy must have been a few years old. Crows feet and a few extra pounds. Had he been any closer, he would have been on her other side.

Gillian took a step back.

"Yes, I know who you are, Mr. Ivanov. I guess the honeymoon is over," she responded in a low voice. On the outside, she was cool and reserved. Inside, she was a freakin' mess.

Her familiarity with him caught Ivanov off guard. "We would like ... ."

She put her right hand up to stop him. "I know.

You're interested in acquiring some diamonds."

He studied her face. "Yes," he replied, curious as to how she knew. He may have misjudged her. "Does this mean you have them? Where are they?" His voice was stern and demanding.

"I know you killed Vladimir," she spouted back. Gillian hoped her hunch would pay off.

He hesitated ever so slightly as his eyes moved down and to the left. He was reliving the whack job. "Why would you say such a thing? I am here on business, Miss Crawford. Your accusations are offensive." This time he stared her straight in the eye.

He was an easy read, she thought, and a liar too. The smugness in his voice made her blood boil. Revenge would be sweet. Gillian positioned the tiny injection pin she had cupped in her hand. A mere bump, Hadley said. His heart would stop in a matter of minutes. But the voices in her head took over. Hadley with his *revenge and dig two graves* speech, and Father Francis with the *Vengeance is Mine* proverb. She struggled to blur them out. One way or another though, he would suffer. If not now, then soon.

"I can tell you if I'm not back to the hotel in thirty minutes, those stones will disappear forever."

"Let's get down to business then. Where are they?" he asked again.

"How does one go about acquiring plutonium, by the way? Have you no moral compass as to the effect of such a sale?"

"My morality is none of your concern."

"You're a criminal of the worst kind. A thief and a

killer," she nearly shouted.

"You look in the mirror lately?"

Gillian studied his expressionless face, and dark, empty eyes. She had found out what she wanted. He was responsible for Sol's death; however the mirror comment struck a nerve.

"Let me get straight to the point," she began. "I'd like to sell them. I wish Vladimir had never given them to me. They've been nothing but trouble."

"Excellent."

"On the other hand, I want to make sure I don't end up dead."

He chuckled at her frankness. "We won't harm you. We just want what is ours."

"All right. Meet me tonight at ten o'clock, outside the maintenance room on the first floor of the hotel. Come alone. That's where the exchange and transfer will take place. Be prepared to wire 5 million to an account in the Caymans. Consider it my finder's fee. They're worth ten times that, so you're getting off cheap. If I suspect anything's amiss, you'll never see those stones again."

He nodded, reached down and picked up his keys, then stepped aside. Gillian put the poison pin in her pocket and walked away. Christine Hansen caught her eye as she passed by.

Brock Hansen walked over to his wife and grabbed her arm. "Let's go."

She grimaced. "What's wrong?"

"If that arrogant bitch thinks we are going to pay for those diamonds, she's more ridiculous than you working for a paycheck. We'll play her little game. But when the time comes ... " He motioned his hand across his throat. "Whewett."

Back in her suite, Gillian grabbed Hadley's satellite phone and placed a call.

"This is as secure as I can get. Now who the bloody hell are you, Harry Stevens?"

"Obviously not Simone Cantore. He's dead. He was the fence Vladimir was planning to use to unload his insurance. I am who I say."

"So where are you now?"

"Headed back from Naples. I've got a couple more places to stop along the way."

"Plan on being back here by ten. Don't be late or you'll miss the emergency evacuation of the hotel. I've lined up a meeting with the alias, Brock Hansen, for the bogus diamond exchange. I'll take care of him. You be on the lookout for Witherspoon, the invalid. He'll be coming out with the help of his entourage, Miss Crenshaw, Glinka - the ogre, and his creepy sidekick. That's your chance. Call him out by name. In the heat of the moment, and with plenty of chaos, people trip up. If you want to take him down, that'll be the time to do so. "

"How will I find you afterwards?"

"I'll be in the parking lot. Good luck."

"Thank you. You too." He rang off. The suddenness surprised her.

Gillian grabbed the first burn phone and texted Finn. *'The meeting is still on for ten. Keep your eyes open and be sharp. We may have visitors.'*

With the second burn phone, she texted Hadley. *'Everything ready for 10? Boat ready?'* He responded immediately. *'Ready and Ready.'*

A few minutes later, she stood naked in the

middle of the shower, the cold water running down from the rain shower head. She was all but numb and needed to be. Eyes closed, breathing shallow, Gillian focused on what needed to be done and said a prayer. As she got out of the shower, and reached for a towel, her laptop buzzed announcing an incoming video call. She threw on a hotel robe and ran to the desk. The image that appeared took her breath away.

Lorelei was sitting in a chair, strapped down, her red hair twisted and frayed, tears running down her cheeks. A five inch strip of silver duct tape covered her mouth. Propped up on her lap was a newspaper. The lens zoomed in and out, to show the date - it was today's. No discriminating items to spot. Suddenly the back side of a man appeared and ripped the tape off her mouth. He held out a sheet of paper in front of her. She peered up at him, like he was telling her something, but Gillian could not see his face, nor make out his voice.

Lorelei sobbed and shook her head. His hand slapped her face, the force of which rocked the chair. The impact left her cheek red with an imprint. Her breathing was hitched, but she managed to focus on the paper and read the message.

"We want the birdcage in exchange for your cousin's life. We will contact you in one hour with the details. Do not contact the police, or any other parties ... or she will die."

Lorelei looked up into the camera. Her eyes pleading, red rimmed from crying. She opened her mouth, stuck her tongue out slightly, and tapped it under her right front tooth, then glanced upward. A hand came into view again and slapped the tape back onto her mouth. The transmission then ended.

Gillian hurried and got dressed; threw on a pair of blue jeans, black tee-shirt and black chucks. She had a pretty good idea where Lorelei was being held. The clue was a small, insignificant movement of her tongue under her front tooth.

Uncle Jack's grandiose hotel had been their playground growing up. When her parents would yell at her to get out of the house, get some fresh air, and go play, she'd run and get Lorelei, and they'd head to the hotel. The building was the perfect place on the island to play hide-and-go-seek. They knew every nook and cranny. The staff let them be, as long as they kept their voices down, for they all knew who Gillian's uncle was.

One summer they were up at the top, playing in the cupola. The room was hot. They wanted to open the windows, but the latches were too high. Gillian took off her shoes. Lorelei got down on her hands and knees so Gillian could climb on her back. It was just the height she needed to reach the clasp. With only her socks on, Gillian slipped and fell on Lorelei's back. Lorelei screamed and hit her mouth on the floor, breaking her front tooth. That was the tooth she tapped in the video. That's where she was. The cupola would provide a bird's eye view of the entire hotel grounds.

The next hour seemed endless. She checked her watch a half dozen times. Her bag was ready. All of her new toys from Hadley were packed, along with money, passports, and a change of clothes. Only a few items remained on the desk. She placed the fake diamonds in a clear plastic bag then dropped them in the black velvet satchel the originals had been in. On the table were the two things Hadley had picked up from the game reserve.

Gillian thought of Sol again, and of happier times, and how much she would miss him. How he must have suffered on his back deck. Alone. Frightened. Bleeding out. Yes, she could do this. She had to do this. What had been set in motion by others, could not be stopped. All she could do was make the most of a bad situation. She paused at her desk, and stared off, her mind empty.

The video call came in. Once again, Lorelei was sitting in the chair, tape still over her mouth. This time Gillian spoke first.

"I need to hear her speak, make sure this isn't recorded, and I want her to have a live video feed of me as well."

The tape was torn off. Gillian heard her whimper.

"I love you, cuz. I'm going to get you out of this." Gillian feigned a smile and lightly bit the tip of her tongue.

Lorelei nodded her head and repeated the gesture.

"I love you, too."

Off screen Gillian overheard a voice with a German accent say, "We have a deal?"

"Yes, but I'm not doing this alone. I'm not stupid. I'll have the birdcage delivered to a boat at the marina at ten o'clock tonight. The canister will only be there for ten minutes. Don't come early, or my delivery guy will be a no show. He'll give you the birdcage, and you give him my cousin's location."

"Vereinbart. Agreed," the voice answered. The

transmission went off.

Gillian looked at her watch - 9:30 p.m. She grabbed the night vision goggles on loan from Hadley and headed to the golf course. She was almost certain poor Finn would be a no show, but she needed to make sure.

Chapter 20

As Gillian made her way through the hotel lobby, she stopped by the courtesy phone and pulled a business card out of her pocket for Agent Dumas. She called his cell.

"Time is running out," he began.

"Ya know, Amir, you're a real piece of work. Here I am calling to tell you where you can find Frederick with his hands in the cookie jar, and you're giving me crap."

"What say you?"

"Head over to the marina. He and his little band of anti-Semitics will be arriving at ten o'clock to pick up your makeshift birdcage. Give 'em a minute to locate your gizmo. You'll know when it's safe to roundup the remaining Jew haters. That's the best delivery on a silver platter you're ever gonna get, Amir. You and your network of Sayanim helpers can say mission accomplished. You're not going to get Hans Vanderhauf, but Frederick Vanderhauf will do. Old age will get his brother soon enough. Pack your bags and go back to Tel Aviv before someone misses you." Click went the phone.

Gillian thoroughly enjoyed putting the son-of-a-bitch in his place. Letting him know she saw right through his subterfuge, gave her tremendous satisfaction. If only the rest of the evening would go so well. The time was 9:45. She headed to the golf course.

Locked inside the hotel's mechanical room, Hadley surveyed his options. The door to the main circuit breaker panel box was open. His eyes scanned down the buss bar until he spotted the 50 amp breaker for the air conditioning unit. In theory what he had decided to do, by creating a high resistance opening, should work. In fifteen minutes, he would be long gone, and his creative assignment would be put to the test. Hadley took a deep breath and exhaled. He grabbed a screwdriver from his hip pocket and steadied his hands. Carefully he stuck the end into the identified lug and loosened the connection from the circuit breaker. He spotted the high voltage wires. One black, the other red. 120 volts of alternating current wouldn't be 180 degrees out of phase much longer. He walked over to a digital thermostat and programmed the air conditioner to kick on at ten o'clock, with a 58 degree setting. Finally, he took an old rag, soaked it with lighter fluid, and delicately wedged the dripping cloth around the wires loosened from the breaker. Hadley left the remaining bottle a few inches away and locked the door on the way out. If all went as planned, at the top of the hour, the thermostat would turn the air conditioning on, an arc between the wires would occur, and the room would be engulfed in flames. Job done.

THE GREEN FOR the eighteenth hole, like the rest of the course, was immaculately groomed and moderately challenging. The last hole sloped gently to the water and was encompassed with bunkers at the front and rear. You could hear the waves lapping the seawall. A tree line of giant Hamiltonii bamboo provided a backdrop for the final hole.

Gillian made her way to the far side and hid behind the bamboo. Standing still, dressed in dark clothes, she blended right in. If only the mosquitoes would leave her alone. With Hadley's night vision goggles on, she settled in and waited.

There he was, lying on the grass over the back side of the bunker. Pauley with a gun. Lucky for him there was no moon tonight. Gillian noticed him tighten the silencer. He was waiting like a spider. Finn had not made it. She shuttered to think what had happened to him. Now the question: who was Pauley waiting for - her, or Finn's killer? One minute later she got her answer.

Yuri Glinka was talking on his cell phone as he strolled up to the green. "This shouldn't take long." He glanced at his wristwatch. "I'm sure I can handle the Crawford dame. The exchange is supposed to take place at 9:45 p.m. I'll call you when I have them. We can check out tonight, as far as I'm concerned. Gotta go."

He walked over to the far side of the green and stared into the wall of bamboo. Gillian froze. She could hear the high pitched sound of a mosquito as it flew around her ears, and landed on her nose. In went the stinger. Gillian flinched and swatted him away. Yuri reached in his pocket, pulled out a flashlight, and shined the beam in her direction. Gillian held her breath and took two steps back. A dried twig broke. His flashlight and gun were on her in a heartbeat.

"Miss Crawford. Such a pleasure to see you again. Those are some interesting glasses you're wearing. Come out, come out, so we can do business."

Gillian hesitated, then took several steps forward until she got to the clearing. She was telling herself, *this is not good. This is really not good.* All she could come up with were the words, "There's been a mistake."

A voice from behind Yuri concurred. "You damn right."

The sound of three muffled shots went off. Two into Yuri's back, the other to his head. He dropped on his knees, then fell flat on his face.

Gillian looked up and spotted Pauley standing on the other side.

"You're here. Not Finn?"

"Finn is dead. And now this piece of shit is too."

"I'm sorry."

"Yeah. Me too. Listen, I gotta run. You got someplace safe to go?"

"Yes, I'll be fine. Thank you. I know those two words are so inadequate, but truly, I owe you."

"Another time, maybe." He winked.

"Addio, amore."

Pauley chuckled and disappeared into the night.

Gillian walked over to the late Chechnyan and nudged him with her foot. He reeked of musk and was stone cold, dead. "That's what you get for feeling me up and smashing my head on the ground, you bastard." She looked at her wristwatch: 9:55 p.m. With the black velvet satchel in hand, Gillian ran to the service entrance on the back side of the hotel.

BROCK HANSEN TURNED the corner to the back hallway and ran into Gillian. He was alone, with a briefcase in hand. He set the black leather case on the hallway table and retrieved his laptop. Gillian looked beyond him and spotted smoke billowing out from under the mechanical room door. Hadley's handy work was right on schedule.

She pointed to the smoke. "Let's make this quick. That looks serious. Here's the number to my account."

"Not so fast. I'd like to checkout what I'm buying first."

Gillian brought the satchel out in the open. He took a step closer. "Do you think I'd be foolish enough to double-cross you? Hurry and open up your hands before we both die of smoke inhalation."

Hansen cupped his hands together as she poured them out, emptying a portion of the bag.

"I must say, they are rather pretty," she added. Gillian stood impatiently as he held one up in his hands. He reached into his jacket pocket and took out a jeweler's loupe.

Hansen cleared his throat and loosened his tie. "Must be the smoke," he said while he held a diamond close to the glass.

Suddenly he clutched his chest and staggered. His eyelids drooped. Gillian noticed the flushness of his face, and beads of sweat across his brow.

He fell down on his knees and leaned slowly against the wall.

"Here's the rest of the jewels." Gillian emptied the remainder of the bag. A small, colorful snake landed on his chest. Hansen jerked. "Just so you know," she continued matter-of-factly, "I laced the diamonds with venom. That's a coral snake, by the way. Not very happy being confined for so long. On contact the venom absorbs into your system. In a few minutes, you'll lose consciousness. The neurotoxin will paralyze your breathing muscles." He was lying very still now. "I guess that's already happened," she paused for effect. "Next up will be a complete shutdown of your lungs. I've got the anti-venom right here." Gillian held up a vial, wiggling it in her hand. "Tell me where Boris Chenkov is, and I'll give it to you.

"You Bitch!" he moaned slightly above a whisper.

"Really. That's all you've got. Come on. Save yourself. Where is he?"

"Suite 203." His eyes rolled back in his head.

"Enjoyed doing business with you," she said sarcastically. "Here's your lifeline. Not that you'll be needing it." She threw the empty glass vial at him and ran down the hall.

At the first sign of a fire alarm, she smashed the glass, pulled down on the lever, and tripped the device.

With no events taking place at this late hour, the majority of the hotel guests were either in their rooms, doing who knows what, or enjoying a night cap in the mahogany paneled, billiard room. No worries. The upside of a charmed life. The penetrating sound of the fire alarm jolted them in to stark reality.

Guests rolled out of the rooms, confused, looking for smoke or flames, and covering their ears. Both staff and guest reactions went from confusion, to panic, to a confused panic in a matter of seconds. At the front desk, the night clerk was on the telephone yelling at the 911 operator as his eyes darted back and forth across the live feed from the security monitors, hunting for answers.

"No, it's not a drill, damnit," he yelled to the operator as he pointed to the monitor. "There ... smoke coming from the HVAC room on the back side of the building, and the main guest elevator in the lobby. Flames? Wait ... yes ... yes. Oh crap. The door to the mechanical room just burst open. The room is engulfed in flames. Sprinklers? No, not yet. We've lost electricity, but the backup generators just kicked in. There's smoke everywhere. Hurry up before someone dies!"

In an instant, the lobby was filled with people piling out the front entrance. The main elevator stopped between floors, as hotel guests pried the doors open then took a six foot leap. A stream of patrons, guided by their illuminated cell phones, filtered out of the darkened stairwell. Loads of men and women converged into the lobby at the same time, all headed in the same direction. The pleasantries of society went out the window as people panicked, and surged for a way out. A chair was thrown through a large plate glass window leading to the veranda, creating another escape route. The surging crowd split in two, as three other large windows fell to a similar fate.

Gillian ran against the flow of guests until she made it to the top floor. The smoke traveling through the elevator shaft had begun to reach the upper levels. She stopped at the emergency exit and caught her breath. Coming out of the doorway, which led to the copula, Gillian spotted Ralph and Rem, running the opposite direction. She waited for them to evacuate the floor, before running to the unmarked entry that led upstairs.

The room was unlocked. Gillian ran in and found Lorelei unconscious, still tied to a chair, lying on the floor. She rushed to her side.

"Lorelei, sweetie, wake up, wake up. We've got to go." She shook her shoulders and smacked her face. "This is going to hurt, sorry." Gillian yanked the tape off her mouth. She moaned. "That-a-girl." She smiled at her as her eyes opened. Lorelei's face lit up when she recognized her cousin. "Here, let me untie you. Listen to me darling. The hotel is on fire. We need to get you out of here. Do you think you can stand?"

Gillian reached around to the back of the chair and untied the rope. Lorelei stood up, rubbed her wrists, and walked over to the window. The view from the top shocked them both. It was now a two-alarm fire. The parking lot was full of emergency vehicles, ambulances, and disheveled hotel guests standing outside in their pajamas, or thrown on clothes. Gillian pointed to the flames shooting out of the top floor of the west wing.

"We need to go. Do you think you can manage?"

"Yes, I think so. But you walk ahead of me down the narrow stairwell, just in case.

When they got to the main hallway, Gillian pointed Lorelei to the emergency exit.

"You go on ahead. I'm going to make sure the floor is clear."

"Shouldn't you let the firemen do that?"

"There's no time. I'll be right behind you. It'll only take a minute. I'll meet you at the side parking lot next to the Washingtonia Palms. Don't worry."

"Okay, but please hurry."

Chapter 21

G illian waited at the top of the stairwell as Lorelei made her way down the three flights of stairs. Only then did she turn and shut the door. At this end of the wing, the air was better with the door closed.

There was a courtesy phone on the wall nearby. Gillian picked up the receiver. *Thank God for a dial tone,* she prayed. Frederick Vanderhauf answered his cell phone on the first ring.

"You're late."

"I've been a little busy."

"I'm at the marina. Where's your guy."

"He's walking up right now."

"I don't see him. If this is a trick, your cousin is dead."

"No, really. Look again. He should be standing next to the boat. Slip 113. A blue 36 foot sail boat." Her voice sounded more and more urgent.

On the other end of the line, Vanderhauf yelled, "Ralph, Rem, check the boat in Slip 113."

A man on the pier in dark pants and hoodie nodded and walked away.

"Okay, lady, where on the boat?"

"Down in the galley. Open the hatch. The birdcage is sitting next to the sink. Now where's my cousin?"

The phone line went dead.

"You get what you deserve," she said to herself.

At the far end of the hallway in the east wing, was Suite 203, the last unit on that floor. Gillian made her way through the smoke to the elevator that serviced both wings. The further she went the worse the conditions. She stopped to wipe her eyes at the half way point. As she peered down the hall, she spotted two men coming out of the last suite. One she recognized as the ogre's creepy sidekick, the other was a man she had not seen before. *Witherspoon. It must be him*, she thought.

"Witherspoon," she yelled at the top of her lungs.

A man dressed in black slacks and dress shirt stopped, turned around, grinned, and ran out the emergency exit. She rushed down the hallway but lost them in the smoke. Gillian ran inside their suite and shut the door. The air quality was better, she was able to catch her breath. Suite 203 was empty. She opened the door to the bedroom where Witherspoon was wrapped in bandages days before. His body was still in the same state, and same position. Was he dead? She shook him, then stopped. A mannequin. The body was a freakin' mannequin. No convalescing Witherspoon. This whole setup was a ruse. As she turned to leave, Gillian spotted the scattered contents on the bathroom floor: wigs, female body suits, dentures, and makeup.

The reality of her discovery hit her like a sucker punch. Helen Crenshaw was Boris Chenkov! The clever bastard. She had been in the same room with him, carried on a conversation with him, was right in his face. How did she miss that? More importantly, how could Harry? It was plain and simple, Harry Stevens was not his nephew. Gillian raced out the door. Who on earth was Harry Stevens?

Local fire marshal, Andrew Bowen, stood next to

the sheriff and admitted, "We've lost her. The building is too far gone. When the blaze reached the wine cellar ... well, that was the turning point. The explosion was too destructive." Bowen gripped the sheriff's shoulder. "Sorry, Sheriff. We'll contain the fire as best we can, but the main building is gone."

In the parking lot, standing side by side, staring at the flames were Sheriff Sam Mitchell, Hadley Stephenson, and Harry Stevens. Their faces were each covered with sweat and ash, their expressions grim.

"Guess I'll be looking for a new job," Hadley said solemnly, studying the destruction caused by his own doing.

The sheriff looked over at Harry, who seemed highly interested in anyone still exiting the building. "Excuse me, are you a guest here?"

"Yes, my name is Philip Albright. I'm here on business."

"Your Philip Albright?" the sheriff asked, not sure he understood him correctly.

"Yes, that's right." He flashed his badge.

"Folks thought you were dead, until yesterday. Do you mind telling me what the hell is going on?"

"I came down here for two things: to help someone I promised to keep safe, and to retrieve something our government likes to keep a lid on."

"Any luck with that?" Sam already knew the answer.

"Not with the first one." Albright glanced down at the ground and kicked the dirt with his shoe. "Solomon Crawford was the first placement assigned to me. That meant something. We had a special connection."

The sheriff skipped right to the second item. "I'm well aware of your missing birdcage, and that you dangled the radioactive material like bait, causing this killing frenzy. Solomon Crawford stabbed to death. A Naples man with this throat slit open believed to be you. And I've just been told there's a dead man on the eighteenth green with a bullet through his head."

"Boris Chenkov, Russian mobster, and all around bad-ass, had one of his goons take out Crawford, as well as Cantore, the Naples guy. Found out he was Crawford's fence. I staged my own crime scene using Cantore's remains, to cast the spotlight elsewhere. Bought me some time until forensics determined otherwise; allowed me to nose around unofficially. I honestly don't know about the guy on the golf course. Maybe you should ask your girlfriend."

"I want you the hell out of my town by morning, and take your radioactive, glow in the dark stuff, with you."

Hadley interrupted. "Hey, isn't that Lorelei heading this way? I think she needs help."

Lorelei staggered towards them but fell. The sheriff rushed to her side and lifted her off her knees. Her face was covered with soot. When she spoke, her voice was but a whisper. "Where's Gillian? Have you seen her? She told me to meet her in the parking lot."

"Wait, where did you see her?" asked the sheriff.

"I was trapped in the cupola, and she got me out."

Each one immediately scanned the parking lot, trying to find her.

"She must still be inside," yelled the sheriff as he

took off running.

The front support beam of the hotel's porte cochere collapsed and blocked the entrance. Fire Marshall Bowen grabbed the sheriff and pulled him back. The heat from the flames was intense. "You can't go in," he yelled. "It's suicide."

"I have to."

"You can't, Sheriff. Whoever's inside ... is gone. There's nothing any of us can do."

Sam Mitchell stood motionless, shoulders hunched, while timbers burned and walls collapsed. His anguished face was covered with soot and sweat. *She can't be gone,* he moaned. "Gillian! Gillian, can you hear me?" he yelled, pacing back and forth. The fireman grabbed him by the shoulders and turned him around. Sam walked with fists clenched, back to where Hadley and Philip Albright were standing. He punched Albright square in the jaw and laid him out.

Hadley didn't bother to lend Albright a hand. He bent over and whispered in his ear, "I think the guy you're looking for just left the building." He pointed to the east exit, then turned and walked away. On the way to his cottage, another explosion occurred. The fireball rose thirty feet in the sky. It came from the direction of the marina. "Score another one for my girl." He was self-satisfied.

BACK AT THE bungalow, Hadley viewed the damage. The roof was singed, but it was still intact. In the rental next door, he heard the bellowing voice of the Texan on the phone.

"Another property will be available soon. I think Katlyn and me will be down here a little longer than we originally planned. This one's a prime piece."

The voice on the other end responded. "I thought we agreed you'd stay on with the agency for another three months."

"You know as well as I do, Callahan, it's time for me to go. You've got guys like Bates and Stevens with fire in their bellies. There's a few ex-agency guys that want to try their hands at real estate development. Southwest Florida seems like a nice enough place to start. If you get in a jam though, you know where to find me."

A BLACK SEDAN pulled up to the burning marina and parked. Amir Dumas rolled down the driver's side window and stared at the nearby pier engulfed in flames. A dozen or so yachts had been destroyed. He was looking for survivors when he spotted Nikolay and Boris Chenkov running down the far side. They were none of his concern, but he was curious. Dumas witnessed them dart back and forth between slips until they settled on a 36 foot express cruiser. He spotted Boris pull a gun out of his jacket, aim, shoot and kill the owner on board. Nikolay untied the ropes then rolled the dead body over the side and into the water. Boris ran over to the helm and started the engine. The boat disappeared into the night.

Amir Dumas, a senior agent of Mossad, spotted Frederick Vanderhauf sitting on a bench, head in his hands, weeping. His grandsons were both dead. There was a certain satisfaction in seeing this monster suffer. The Crawford lady was right. Time would take his brother soon enough. He leaned out the window, aimed and fired one shot. Vanderhauf rolled slowly off the bench and fell to the ground. The tinted window went up and his car pulled away.

Chapter 22

Francesca Arnman arrived at the Geneva Branch of Banco del Isle, thirty minutes before noon. Dressed in a pencil thin dress, dark gray with stripes, black stiletto heels, long, blonde hair tied back with a red scarf, she appeared cool, confident, and ready for business.

The Banco del Isle was located in the downtown financial district. Like most money center banks, the financial institution had its own International Department, the location of which was separate from the main lobby, and was divided into global regions to assist with their clients unique needs. After a brief conversation with the receptionist, Francesca was directed to the corner office belonging to Mr. Claude Devaro, an assistant manager, specializing in Russian and Eastern European clientele.

Mr. Devaro stood courteously when she approached. He was a middle aged man, single, not much to look at. His mundane job of processing international wire transfers was made more enjoyable, thankfully, by females who frequented his office. Serious money seemed to go hand in hand with beautiful women. Women who would otherwise never give him the time of day. When they moved money around the world, however, they needed him.

"Good Morning, Miss. How may I help you?"

"Francesca Arnman. I received notice of an incoming wire this morning." Her voice was soft and low. Her English was good. Boarding school good.

"Let me grab your file. Yes, here we go." He opened a legal size folder lying on his desk. "Now if I can get you to enter your ten digit pin, followed by your hand print on the scanner, we can proceed." He turned the dual keypad/scanner towards her.

Her mind drifted back to six weeks ago, recalling the moment when her prints were taken. She had stepped into the salon at the Boca Grande Hotel, for a mani-pedi, the day before the place burnt down. Her hands were spread out on a glass plate, under the dryer. That charming, little beauty parlor was where she got to know the woman who would become her benefactor. The transaction was a simple pro quo, she was told, but would change her life. The memory of their conversation had been a constant in her mind. *Why her? Why pick her? Could this woman see through her facade? Realize how trapped she felt? Was their meeting providence, or luck?* Either way, she jumped at the chance. Francesca had used the chaos and confusion of the fire to escape. It was a leap of faith for her to make this trip, not knowing whether or not the woman had gone through with her plan. For all she knew she had died in the fire, along with Boris and the others.

Francesca looked up and smiled. She had smurfed money numerous times in the past for the Chenkov family; large amounts laundered through the global financial markets. Never for herself, though. With this incoming wire, she'd be able to disappear for a good long while. No more jet-setting, but at least she would be free; no longer someone's possession. Never that again. Her hand shook ever so slightly as she reached for the pad and scooted closer to the desk.

Mr. Devaro waited for security confirmation before he continued. "Excellent, Miss Arnman. Now, per the instructions received by our client, the twenty-four million is to be split three ways. Eight million to an account of your choosing. The second eight to an existing account, with the remaining eight to The Lady of the Lakes Orphanage in Boca Grande, Florida, United States. Now, if I can get your authorization to release the funds, I'll have you out of here in time for lunch." He smiled, adjusted his reading glasses, then completed the transaction with his keyboard.

The Orphanage. *That confirmed the story she was told,* Francesca recalled. The woman wanted to make sure they were taken care of. She had hired her to act on her behalf; in case ... in case she didn't make it. Francesca guessed she hadn't. *She should never have gone up against them*, she thought sadly. The far reach of the Chenkov Family was too much. But now here she was doing the same thing. *Escape or die*, she reasoned. It was a simple choice.

Fifteen minutes later, she stood outside the bank and grabbed a burn phone from her large alligator purse. She doubted there was a recipient to receive the message, but did as she was instructed and texted the word, *'done'* to the number she was given.

Francesca then hailed a cab.

"Airport, please. Quantum Airways, step on it and keep your eyes on the road." As they drove across the bridge, Francesca rolled down the window and threw the burn phone into the Rhone River.

Inside her large bag, she pulled out a black shirt,

leather jacket and jeans. The first thing that came off though was the wig. The long blonde hair, a perfect match to her original tresses, soon went out the window. Underneath was a short, black cut she was still getting use to. Her hands ran through the spiky layers trying to put some fluff in her 'do. She caught a glimpse of the cabby's eyes in the mirror.

"Hey creeper, what did I say? Keep your eyes on the road. How much longer?"

"Five minutes tops."

As she wiggled out of her tight fitting dress, the cabby glanced from road to mirror and tried not to crash.

Epilogue

Father Flannigan greeted the local mailman at the Gasparilla Island Post Office in the middle of town. To describe it as tiny would be an understatement. The government office was the oldest building on the island, and was commonly used as a landmark, as in, go to the Post Office and hang a left. The priest enjoyed the daily stroll from his parish to downtown, by way of a children's path, lined with trees. The route was shady and pleasant. Today's post was light. Only a few advertisements and a utility bill.

"Good morning, Father. Hope you're doing well?" the postman asked in genuine concern.

"No complaints," he responded, but added nothing further. The last six weeks had been difficult. His gift of gab had gone silent.

Father Flannigan hesitated as he walked out the door. In the mix of the glossy flyers was a picture postcard of the Sistine Chapel, addressed to him, with nothing further added. No comments, anecdotes, nothing. He checked the postmark. It was stamped ten days ago from Rome. He tried to recall if any of his parishioners had mentioned a trip. He slipped the postcard in his shirt pocket then strolled back to St. Michael's.

How nice it would be to go back to the Vatican this summer, he thought; *recharge his batteries. He was definitely going to look into that.* The last month and a half had been emotionally challenging. The fire had been devastating. The hotel was destroyed. A man was found shot to death on the golf course. And part of the marina exploded.

Several members of the community had lost their lives, leaving an empty void he struggled with daily; Gillian Crawford being among them. No one would ever know of her philanthropic works, their theological discussions and the mental struggles she endured. He missed her wit and charm. Things would never be the same.

Gillian was last seen running in the hallway of the east wing looking for trapped guests after rescuing her cousin, Lorelei Hampsted. Lorelei survived, Gillian was consumed by the fire. Her gold signet ring with the initials GAC was found next to the HVAC room on the first floor, where the fire marshal determined was ground zero.

When he reached the church courtyard, he laid the postcard and mail down on a garden bench and sat down in the shade. He smiled when he recalled his attempt at paint-by-numbers of the Sistine Chapel. That one had been a lesson in patience. Gillian had schooled him on that. He chuckled. Father Flannigan reached for the postcard and flipped it over several times in his hands. It was thicker than most. He noticed the tiny captioned words on the back side: *'Vatican Guards.'* Hmm, someone had gotten that wrong.

He studied it closer. No, they hadn't. Someone had painstakingly glued two cards together.

He took his pocket knife out of his trousers and pried two corners apart. Inside was a small black and white photograph of a beautiful young woman, with blond hair, in a black trench coat, high heels, and a big smile. He studied her face. It was Gillian. On the back side of the photograph were the words, *'Faith first, then deeds. Yes, Father. I'm working on that.'*

Father Francis Flannigan's heart leaped from within. He stared at the photo, as his eyes welled up with tears. From his pants pocket he took out a lighter and set them all on fire. He watched them burn until all that remained were ashes.

Ashes to ashes. Dust to dust. In sure and certain hope of the Resurrection to Eternal Life, through our Lord Jesus Christ.

He smiled and began to hum. It was well with her soul, and his too.

THE END

Pulp21-Who We Are

Pulp21 was established in 2013 with the objective of publishing compelling stories brought more to life with photographs - a unique and diverting way to Picture What You Read®. The creative writing of the early 20th century provided the springboard for this new generation of pulps: riveting short novels, captivating photographs, variety of genres. For more information about this new niche format, visit us at:

picturewhatyouread.com

pulp21.com

YouTube Channel: Picture What You Read®

Available in both eBook and Paperback.

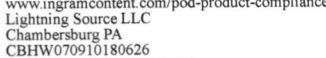